ZACH KRYTON
THRILLER

PEGASUS

JOSH
FRANCIS

Copyright 2019

Josh Francis

ISBN: 978-0-6487025-0-4 (paperback)

Published by Red Diamond
www.red-diamond.com.au

Sign up to the reader's group

This story is fictional!

Cover media by Onur Aksoy – Great work Onur!
www.onegraphica.com

Also By Josh Francis

Pegasus – The Zach Kryton Introductory Series (Book 1).

Poseidon – The Zach Kryton Introductory Series (Book 2).

Phoenix – The Zach Kryton Introductory Series (Book 3).

Battle Rhythm – The military-inspired personal planning, discipline and motivation guide (The Camouflage Series Book 1).

Centre of Gravity – The principles soldiers use to think, act and achieve success (The Camouflage Series Book 2).

Under the Pump – Anecdotes of a service station operator.

Follow Us

You can find other publications and join our conversations on social media. This will keep you up to date with upcoming books and allow you to share ideas. Feel free to contribute!

INSTAGRAM

FACEBOOK

AMAZON

Please leave an honest review on Amazon. This helps to tailor and improve the content of what we produce.

Contents

1

Dili Harbour, TIMOR-LESTE
0330 hours

The low hum of the outboard motor quietly drifted through the warm night air.

The three men aboard the small inflatable raft sat in silence, their boat and its contents occasionally illuminated by the waxing crescent moon that shone down through the gathering storm clouds. The coxswain – the person responsible for steering the boat – gently manipulated the throttle attached to the handle of the outboard motor. His vision was enhanced by the night vision goggles – NVGs – which he wore atop his head. The tubular lenses covered both his eyes, allowing him to see the world through a dull green glow.

He had a pistol by his side – ready if needed.

The man at the stern of the small boat also wore NVGs.

As the coxswain slowly reduced speed, now almost to a crawl, the man at the front of the boat removed an L-shaped torch from his coat pocket and brought it up to his chest. He depressed the switch on the top of it twice in quick succession.

He waited, staring intensely at the wharf where he had just aimed his torch.

Nothing happened.

He showed no concern for the bright light which had just emanated from his torch.

He didn't need to, for the torch was an infrared illuminating device, which could only be seen by someone wearing NVGs, just like his.

He arched his neck forward in the manner one does when trying to focus more closely on something. He manipulated his thumb over the switch again. Just as he was about to press it once more, a singular bright light broke through the green and black glow which had filled his vision through the tubular lenses.

1

It flashed again.

And again.

He placed the torch back into his coat pocket, turned his head and faced his coxswain. Without uttering a word, he nodded once and pointed his hand towards the origin of the bright light.

Three singular flashes. That was the signal he had been expecting.

The coxswain nodded back and gently turned the throttle to increase speed.

The boat and its three crew were now moving directly towards the side of the harbour's wharf, less than a few hundred metres away.

At their speed, slow enough to ensure the revving of the motor didn't unnecessarily alert anyone to their presence, they would be alongside the concrete wharf in little over two minutes.

Waiting for them on the wharf were two other men, one of who had held the torch to give the approach signal. This fourth man, as the Signaller, also wore NVGs, and as the small boat approached, he moved down a set of stairs which led down to a small landing at the water's edge. He kneeled just as a small rope was thrown to him, and he used it to help pull the boat flush against the landing.

The lead crew man jumped onto the landing, took hold of the rope and quickly tied it to a small cleat. The other two crew members purposefully jumped out of the boat and began to remove the boxes that had been their cargo.

Up at the top of the stairs, the fifth man intensely looked up and down the wharf, his back to his companions and monitoring for anyone or anything that might disturb their activities. He was shorter and thinner than all his companions and stood next to an old looking small white truck. A green fabric canopy covered the frames over its rear tray.

It wouldn't look out of place on the streets of Dili, and certainly not down by the harbour where cargo vessels frequently unloaded their goods onto similar-looking vehicles.

With the ease of seasoned professionals, the two boxes were rushed up the stairs in quick succession and quietly placed into the back of the truck. Without saying a word, the coxswain and the second crew member softly shook hands with the lead crew member, and then quickly returned to their boat.

The lead crew member stood next to the remaining two men next to the rear of the truck and looked at them intensely. An imposing figure, he was taller than them and of stocky build. All three of them wore dark coloured cargo pants and olive-green tactical style coats with many pockets, similar to those worn by hikers.

"Any issues?" he whispered in Mandarin.

They both shook their heads.

"No, Boss," they replied simultaneously.

He looked back down to the waterline and saw that his companions had already started driving the boat out of the harbour and into the darkness. He paused for a moment to gather his thoughts while the other two men moved to the front of the truck and jumped inside, the shorter man taking a position in the driver's seat, while the Signaller sat next to him in the middle seat.

The Boss removed a small mobile phone from his coat pocket, pressed a few buttons and placed it to his left ear.

The dial tone rang twice before a female voice on the other end spoke, also in Mandarin.

"Status?" she asked.

"Landed," he replied.

"Acknowledged," came the voice from the other end of the phone before an audible click indicated the termination of the call.

The man placed the phone back into his coat pocket and proceeded to join his companions in the left-hand side passenger seat.

"Let's go," he instructed the Driver.

The three men sat in silence as the Driver made his way along the wharf, the headlights deliberately turned off. They approached the gate that guarded the entrance to the wharf and stopped a few metres shy of it. The guard box was empty, as was common during the evening where virtually no activity occurred at that part of the harbour.

The Boss and the Signaller jumped down from the front of the truck and quickly moved in silence to the gate, where the truck had passed through less than twenty minutes earlier. A small electronic numbered keypad sat on the right-hand pole which was part of the frame of the gate. The Signaller entered a four-digit code, just as he had done to get in earlier. The Boss stood next to him, looking around to observe for potential threats.

The keypad beeped twice and a small red light flickered next to the buttons.

Nothing happened.

The Signaller tried entering the code again, but again nothing happened.

"What's wrong?" asked the Boss, his voice clearly indicating that he was becoming nervous.

"I don't know. It worked before," he replied, still playing with the buttons but with no success.

The Boss looked to the Driver, who was impatiently tapping his fingers on the steering wheel and staring at the Signaller, almost willing the gate to open.

It didn't.

They tried again.

Still nothing.

The Boss looked down at his watch, then back at his companion.

"We need this opened. Now."

2

On the other side of the wharf, inside the rear of a small office that jutted out to the side of a large storage warehouse, the English Premier League match of the day played on a small television screen. Deeply engrossed were two young Timorese men, both eager soccer fans, and both at that moment the sole security officers for the wharf.

The majority of the goods that the Timor-Leste government traded came through and were stored at this small harbour in the nation's capital. Yet the government had deigned it as not requiring any great level of security.

That costs money.

Carlos, the older and more experienced of the two guards, stood from his small stool and gestured at the television with both arms as Tottenham Hotspur made another attacking run towards the Arsenal goal line. His companion, a wiry young lad barely out of his teens named Alberto, smiled as they both verbally encouraged the striker as he dodged several defenders before his thumping goal attempt sailed well over the Arsenal goalkeeper's outreached hands.

Both guards slumped back into their seats in dismay as Carlos placed his hands over his head in frustration. The score would remain nil-all as the two teams headed to the locker rooms upon the referee blowing his whistle indicating half time.

The London derby was always a favourite between the two friends, both Tottenham supporters, who had known each other since Alberto had helped fend off a bully who was attacking Carlos when they were in primary school together. Although he carried a babyface, had a very thin frame and was younger than the bully, his actions that day had earnt Alberto the name *Cara Durão*, or *tough guy* in Portuguese.

Although the native language of the Timorese is Tetum, the remnants of Portuguese colonisation reached far into the language and culture of the Timorese people.

"It's fine, I think we can have them in the second half!" Carlos said to his friend.

5

"Yes," replied Alberto, "I think we are still the stronger team."

Alberto stood up from his seat and removed a pack of cigarettes from his pocket. He looked at his friend with raised eyebrows in an offering gesture, holding out his hand and the packet it contained.

"No. I'm good," said Carlos.

"Okay. I'm off to do the rounds," Alberto said as he walked towards the door and outside.

Alberto lit a cigarette and stood for a moment to allow his eyes to adjust to the night sky. The harbour wharf wasn't particularly well-lit, but even so, the consequences of having spent the last forty-five minutes inches away from the television screen forced Alberto to rub his eyes in order to adjust his vision.

Carlos sat back in his seat and looked over to the small computer monitor sitting on the corner of the desk. He noticed a small flashing light on the screen. He rolled his chair over to the desk, took the mouse into his right hand and double-clicked on the screen. The computer indicated that there was a problem with the front gate, due to an incorrect code being placed into the keypad. He thought it strange. They weren't expecting any deliveries or people that night.

The warm air swept across Alberto's face, and he added to it by exhaling his first breath of tobacco filled air. He had only been working as a guard for a few months. Carlos had secured him the role as a secondary night guard, which suited them both fine as it allowed them free access to the Harbour Master's satellite television feed and the soccer games that came with it. Although they diligently conducted their duties over their twelve-hour shift, their main focus was always on the European soccer games that played out all night long.

"Hey," said Carlos, sticking his head out the door and looking at his friend.

"Can you check the front gate; the computer says there's a problem."

"Okay," replied Alberto, "I'll go and take a look."

Carlos couldn't provide any more details. He was not very computer literate, Alberto even less so. He knew how to click the mouse on a few key parts of the security software, but the formal training they had received for their role consisted of the issuing of both a uniform and the remote control to the television.

Carlos certainly didn't know how to click over to the CCTV feed that would have clearly shown the static truck at the front gate, and the two Chinese men standing in front of it trying to access the keypad.

Alberto walked around the large warehouse, guided by a few dimly lit tubular lights atop of the poles, similar to street lights, which struggled to give more than a few metres of illumination in any direction.

He continued to inhale on his cigarette just as the first few drops of an expected rainstorm fell on his head. He looked to the sky and sighed. Although the drops weren't cold, being wet would make watching the second half of the match uncomfortable. The few drops turned into a steady downfall as he slowly jogged the ninety or so metres to the front gate. He decided to stick to the side of the warehouse as it afforded him a little more protection from the rain. However, he moved while keeping his eyes on the ground in an effort to avoid tripping over any of the numerous obstacles that were stacked against the wall, such as the old wooden pallets and boat engine parts that littered the wharf.

This meant that he approached the front gate without seeing the truck, or its occupants, and didn't notice them until he was at the corner edge of the warehouse and only a few metres from the rear of the truck.

Despite the increased intensity of the rain reducing his vision, Alberto could see two figures standing by the side of the gate.

"Hello," he shouted in Tetum.

There was no reply.

He strained his neck, trying to get a better look at what was going on, but trying to avoid putting his whole body out into the rain.

He looked back down the side of the warehouse from where he had just come, wondering what he should do now. He looked back at the two men at the gate. He could hear voices slowly getting louder, but they were in a language he could not understand.

"Are you okay?" he said, but this time in English.

Still no reply came from the two men next to the gate.

Alberto decided that he would rather see the second half of the match wet than not at all, so he steeled himself for the inevitable drenching he was about to receive and began to walk quickly over to where the men were standing.

The noise of sloshing footsteps alerted the Signaller, who looked up just as Alberto was passing the closed passenger door of the truck.

The unexpected presence of the young Timorese startled the Chinese man for a moment before he quickly regained his composure.

"Boss!" he whispered, looking at his companion next to him while motioning with his head to the direction where Alberto was coming from.

7

The Boss quickly looked over his shoulder, identified where Alberto was, then looked back at the Signaller while motioning for him to continue trying to get the code to work. He then placed himself deliberately between the Signaller and Alberto, attempting to conceal their actions. He stared at Alberto, who was now standing only a few paces from him.

"What's going on?" asked Alberto curiously, again speaking in English.

"We're just leaving," replied the large Chinese man in heavily accented broken English.

Alberto stood with his hands on his hips, attempting to see what the other Chinese man was doing next to the keypad. The rain was falling heavily now, and as he hadn't been trained in any aspects of security, he had no idea what to do. All he knew was that he was saturated and that he wanted to get back to watch the rest of the soccer.

"I'll go and get someone," he said, genuinely wanting to help but unsure as to what he could do.

He turned and took a few paces, intending to go and seek Carlos' assistance.

He didn't make it far.

Two shots in quick succession from the barrel of a QSZ-92, a Chinese made nine-millimetre pistol up until now concealed in the coat pocket of the Boss, struck Alberto in his upper back. The sound of the weapon firing was muffled by the falling rain.

Alberto fell to his knees in pain, unsure as to why he was suddenly unable to walk.

In shock, he attempted to crawl towards the corner of the warehouse.

The Boss walked up to him, his right hand holding the pistol extended out in front of him.

There was no doubt about his intentions.

Alberto was now on his back, looking up at the intimidating Chinese man standing over him. He placed his hands up and out in front of him, pleading for his life. Just as the Boss was about to fire another bullet into Alberto, a clanging noise loudly emanated from near the side of the warehouse, about thirty metres away.

The Boss looked up and squinted, trying to peer into the little amount of light that illuminated the warehouse exterior. He saw a figure crouching down by an old oil drum, a terrified look on the person's face.

It was Carlos.

He had come to bring his friend an old umbrella that had been kept in the security office for the purpose of avoiding getting wet while doing the security rounds. Instead, he had witnessed Alberto being shot, and could now see him dying on the concrete ground in the pouring rain.

He knew there was nothing he could do to help.

Carlos stood up, turned and ran.

He ran as fast as he could.

A whizzing sound went sailing past his head as he ran away, forcing him to jump to his right and fall over a wooden pallet carelessly placed on the ground. It was a bullet from the Bosses' pistol, aimed directly at his head. The bullet veered off course because the intended target was out of the effective range of that particular weapon. An accurate strike would likely have been lethal.

Already compromised, there was no need for further silence.

"Get that gate open," the Boss shouted to the Signaller in Mandarin.

He looked at the Driver, who had now exited the truck and was standing next to him over the prostrate Alberto.

His pistol was also drawn.

"After him," instructed the Boss to the Driver, and the two men sprinted in pursuit of Carlos.

The frightened Timorese ran through a partially open door and into the warehouse. He stopped for a moment, looking for anywhere to hide. The warehouse was dark, and he couldn't see any other escape option. He certainly couldn't go back through the way he had just come. He ran into the depths of the warehouse and sought any cover he could find.

His pursuers soon arrived at the same door. They entered as a synchronised pair, their weapons out in front of them, safety's off and scanning their front for a target.

Just as professionals are trained to do.

They moved slowly and deliberately. There was almost no light, apart from a few small windows that allowed some of the dim external lights to shine through. They had left their NVGs in the truck, so they would have to rely on all their senses.

The Boss took the lead, and they moved along the interior wall. Their vision was slowly adapting to the darkness of the warehouse, and they were now able to see some faint outlines. The warehouse was full of storage containers and numerous other cargoes. They continued to move forward, their pistols held in two hands in bended arms and up in front of their faces, ready to take an opportune shot.

9

Crash – BANG.

The sudden loud clanging noise startled the two men, and they both turned to their left in quick succession, their pistols gripped tightly in their now extended arms, ready to engage the threat.

A small cat miaowed as it spotted the intruders. It had knocked over some loose tins as it had jumped onto a medium size wooden box sitting alone within the warehouse. The Chinese men lowered their weapons and looked at each other, likely both wondering how it was neither of them had shot the feline that was now moving in small circles in the middle of the box, preparing to lie down to see out the remainder of the storm in the dryness of the warehouse.

The Boss scanned the warehouse intensely, but couldn't see anything significant. He applied the safety to his pistol and returned it to his coat. He decided that there were now more important things to be concerned with and time was against them.

"Let's go," he said to his companion.

They moved quickly out the door that they had come through and sprinted back to the truck. The Signaller had managed to get the gate open and was now kneeling over Alberto. The two men quickly joined him, and both looked down at the body lying prone in front of them in a pool of blood.

Alberto was dead.

"Do we continue?" asked the Driver, looking at the Boss.

"Yes," came the curt reply.

All three men jumped back into their original seats.

With headlights on, the truck drove at speed through the gate, up a hill leading to the main streets and into the Dili night.

The rain continued to pour down as Carlos huddled in the far corner of the inside of the warehouse. The noise of the water hitting the corrugated iron roof had masked his heavy breathing. He stayed there for half-an-hour, trying to comprehend what he had just seen, and still believing that there were two assailants after him. An hour later the rain ceased and the warehouse was eerily quiet again, as it was most nights.

Carlos finally gathered the courage to leave his hiding position and go back outside. The early signs of morning twilight were starting to appear in the east, and the clouds had cleared. He moved over to where the body of his friend was. Carlos looked down at his childhood friend, disbelieving that he was now holding his lifeless body in his arms.

A range of emotions and thoughts started surging through him.

What had happened?
Who were those men?

He looked around, looking for anything or anyone to help him. Tears formed in his eyes. It was still going to be an hour before the next team of guards came on duty. Fear was now the main emotion he felt. Carlos gently laid his friend's head back on the ground, stood up and ran out through the gate and into the streets of Dili.

3

The attack came fast and furious, and almost caught Zach Kryton by surprise. He parried the right cross punch with his left hand, instantly bringing his own right arm up and covering his head, cupping the back of it with his palm in case the left-hand hook that his attacker followed up with should make its way around to the back of his neck.

It didn't, and with the attempted strike successfully blocked he instantly pushed the attacker back with an open palm into the chest, allowing just enough space to open up to follow on with a well-placed front kick to his opponent's lower stomach.

This naturally forced his opponent to drop his head, and Kryton wasted no time in closing the gap and wrapping his right arm around the back of his opponent's exposed neck, bringing his forearm under the flailing man's throat.

In a desperate bid to counter the move, the man threw his right arm up into the air, aiming for Kryton's head in an effort to release his attacker's grip.

However, this was exactly what Kryton wanted him to do. Both men were of similar height and build. Just under six feet, and close to ninety kilograms, all muscle. It was an even pairing physically – but not skills-wise.

With his left hand, Kryton took hold of his opponent's right wrist and drew the arm out to full extension, and in one sweeping motion pushed it across his own face to his right side, simultaneously pushing down on the back of the head, using it as a fulcrum which forced his opponent to twist around and fall onto his backside. He was now sitting in front of Kryton. A crumpled mess, with his wrist well held in a gooseneck lock by the superior fighter who was now inflicting pain on the poor lad.

"Give?" demanded Kryton, his stance ensuring that he had complete control over any movement his opponent tried to make.

"Give," came the pitiful reply of an opponent soundly defeated, his only desire being to avoid any further stress being placed onto his completely immobilised wrist.

In one smooth motion, Kryton released the grip and squatted down to place his arm under his opponent's shoulder, bringing him to his feet again as if offering an elderly person assistance to get off of a bus.

The two men faced each other, Kryton looking at his opponent with an air of authority, but also respect.

"Good?" he asked quietly and with sincerity.

"Yes, Sensei," came the reply, the younger lad standing with a sheepish smile on his face.

Kryton smiled, slapped him on the side of the arm and motioned for him to join the rest of his colleagues, who had been standing in a semi-circle watching the two men spar.

There were maybe fifteen young officer cadets standing in front of him, and with quick precision they all moved into two ranks, facing their instructor. Kryton had just finished a class teaching Ju-Jitsu to trainees at the Royal Military College at Duntroon – RMC. Australia's version of West Point. They would be graduating in a few months, and would then proceed into the various Corps of the Australian Army.

"So, simple movements with controlled aggression is the key. Yes, the move was a bit showy, but it's still effective, agree?" he asked the eager young students.

"Osu," they replied in unison, the word of affirmation universally used by martial arts students.

"Good. Class – dis-missed," he said in a professional military tone, giving a small bow to his students in a sign of respect, which was diligently reciprocated.

These cadets cherished the opportunity to be learning from such an exponent of the martial art. Most had heard the stories. The former sergeant with a distinguished career in special operations intelligence. Service in Iraq, Afghanistan, and Timor-Leste – just like many Australian soldiers had in the past twenty years.

Those were only the stories they knew of.

Kryton moved off of the mats to allow the cadets to pick them up and stack them back into the position against the gymnasium wall. The RMC basketball club had waited patiently, and now they wanted their turn on the floor. He moved over to the side of the court and took a seat on the front wooden bleacher, reaching into his gym bag and removing a bottle of water.

"Good to be back?" asked a voice from over his shoulder.

Kryton took a sip from the bottle, keeping his eyes forward and watching the missed lay-up attempt from one of the cadets.

He adjusted his position and turned to look up at the suited man sitting on the bleacher behind him.

"I saw you during the middle of the class," he said drolly, countering the suit's attempt to give the impression he had caught him off guard.

Kryton removed the top of his Gi and replaced it with a plain black cotton polo shirt, neatly folding the Gi top and placing it into his bag. He stood up from his seat and looked around the gymnasium floor.

"Well, new cadets – but the rest looks the same," he said, answering the man's question.

Kryton was referring to the two years he was posted as an instructor at RMC, a position he had gone kicking and screaming into, but that he ultimately enjoyed none the less. He had no choice but to go, as his time in the deployable units of the army had been interrupted as a result of an IED blast in Kabul, and the military doctor's subsequent decision to place him on the medically unfit register.

A decision Kryton had vehemently disagreed with.

His career over at the stroke of a pen.

He had been allowed to stay in the army reserves, however, and made a few extra dollars doing instruction for officer cadets here and there. His military pension made up the remainder of his income, and he did the odd bodyguard job for some B-grade celebrity who nobody knew or would want to hurt anyway.

It helped to make him still feel valued.

"What can I do for you, Jonas?" Kryton asked in a familial tone, smiling and shaking the suit's hand.

He placed the last of his contents into his bag and threw the strap over his shoulder.

"We need your help," replied the suited man seriously, having moved down the bleachers to stand next to his old colleague. "How's your health?"

"Great," replied Kryton sarcastically, "just like it was the day they kicked me out."

Jonas smiled sympathetically. He knew the full story. They had served together after all, on more than one occasion.

"Well, we have something that needs you," he said hopefully.

Kryton just looked at Jonas.

"I'm done with that. Besides, what would the service want from me?" he asked, using the shorthand used by those inside to refer to the Australian foreign spy agency and Jonas' current employer, the Australian Secret Intelligence Service – ASIS.

"Something important has come up, and we need to brief you," Jonas said succinctly, not wanting to elaborate on classified details in an open setting, maintaining standard security practices.

Kryton scoffed, looked at Jonas and shook his head.

"I'm done," he said patiently and turned to walk away. "Come on, I'll buy you a beer at least, the mess is probably open."

Jonas stood in place and watched as Kryton took a few paces towards the door of the gymnasium.

"Pegasus rang," he said calmly.

Kryton stopped in his tracks.

He turned his head and looked at Jonas intensely.

He sighed and looked out onto the court where one of the cadets landed an impressive three-point shot from above the key.

Oh.

Jonas reached into his breast pocket and pulled out a plane ticket. He walked over to Kryton and handed it to him.

"You're on the plane first thing in the morning."

Kryton took hold of the ticket.

"How could you be sure I'd say yes?" he asked Jonas.

"Because you didn't leave all of this on your own terms, and I know that I'd want to. Maybe this is a way that you can."

Kryton tapped the ticket on the inside of his palm. Many thoughts ran through his head.

He looked up at Jonas and slowly nodded.

"Okay – I'll go."

4

Kryton looked out of the window and down to the beautiful blue water below. The sun's reflection glistened off of the wave tops and back up to the plane flying at thirty-thousand feet above, shimmering like a disco ball. The magnificent sight wasn't enough to distract Kryton from his deep thought process.

Nor was the smooth voice of the flight attendant.

A hand tugged on his right arm, bringing him back into the present. His left hand instinctively reached down and tightly grabbed hold of the intrusion. Years of conducting drills in hand-to-hand combat had sharpened his reaction time as well as his fine motor skills.

He looked up and saw a large bespectacled man looking back at him from the seat adjacent; eyes wide and obviously shocked at how quickly Kryton had moved.

"Do you want anything?" asked the man, pointing to the aisle of the plane with his trembling free hand.

Kryton looked back at him confused, before looking up to see a pretty young lady looking down at him, smiling. She wore the uniform of an Airnorth flight attendant – a dark knee-length skirt with a white top, buttoned-up just enough to leave something to the imagination.

"Would you like something, sir?" she asked, motioning to the trolley loaded with drinks.

Kryton let go of the man's hand. The poor chap immediately rubbed at it, returning his attention to the small display screen on the seat in front of him, regretting his decision to touch his neighbour.

"Uh, no thanks," said Kryton politely.

The flight attendant continued to smile and moved the trolley further down the aisle of the plane.

"Sorry," said Kryton to his neighbour, who was still rubbing his hand.

Although nearly twice the size of Kryton, the overweight man was clearly timid. He looked out of the corner of his glasses and nodded a few times, just wanting to be left alone to watch the end of the movie.

Kryton looked back out of the window and stifled a small chuckle.

He quickly returned to his previous thoughts.

He remembered the first time he had flown this particular route. Only that time it wasn't in an air-conditioned plane but in the back of a noisy Royal Australian Air Force C-130 Hercules transport plane. After voting for independence from Indonesia in 1999, the people of what was then known as East Timor suffered brutally in a wave of violence initiated by pro-Indonesian militias. The U.N. asked Australia to lead an international military force to restore order. As a young paratrooper, Kryton took his first steps on foreign soil as part of that operation, known as the International Force East Timor – INTERFET.

He thought specifically about the flight he took several years after that first deployment, this time as a hardened sergeant seconded to ASIS and as part of a special operations team charged with identifying and capturing an anti-government rebel leader.

The early years of the fledgling nation, now using the Tetum name for East Timor of *Timor-Leste,* had been difficult. International forces had been asked to stay far longer than initially anticipated. In the late 2000's, almost half of the new Timor-Leste Army had deserted and fled into the dense jungle hills, taking their weapons with them. From there they vowed to overthrow the government.

Kryton's team had been tasked to gather intelligence on the whereabouts of the rebels and to help remove the threat any way necessary. His specific role was to enter the villages and exploit the established human intelligence network, built painstakingly over the years following the initial INTERFET landings. Once the INTERFET operation and the subsequent U.N. peacekeeping effort took over, the army had handed that network over to the service to keep on ice, should it ever be needed again.

"Ladies and Gentlemen, we'll soon begin our descent into Dili. Please ensure your tray tables and seats are in the upright position," came the voice over the speaker, the head flight attendant informing the passengers that they would soon be landing.

Kryton looked out of the window and down upon the green hills and jungle below that slowly crept up as the plane steadily bled altitude. He could remember the smells of the villages that he had spent weeks living

17

in, gaining the trust of the local population and moving covertly through the hills with his two-man support team.

Their cover – the guise for being in a certain place at a certain time – had been as an NGO team providing medical aid in the remote villages, which they had done so to the great appreciation of the many people they had assisted. They had been able to do this because his team were qualified special forces soldiers, and advanced medical training is a key part of their wider skillsets.

"Cabin staff, please be seated for landing," said the pilot.

Kryton continued to look down towards the ground. They were now low enough that he could clearly see the outline of the rooves of the village houses and huts. They were made with an eclectic mix of wood, corrugated iron, and ceramic tiles. He recalled having spent many evenings sharing dinner at the house of a young Timorese man whose information had proved invaluable in determining the location of the leader of the rebels.

The plane tilted from side to side as the pilot made his final approach from the west to the single runway that was Dili International Airport. Kryton looked to the right at his neighbour, who was gripping both the hand rests like his life depended on it.

At least we're not getting shot at, mate, Kryton thought to himself, thinking of the last time he had flown into Afghanistan.

He looked back down out the window, the plane now flying parallel to the coastline. The thud of the wheels locking into place echoed over the noise of the engines.

The intelligence provided by that young man, obtained at the direction of Kryton and often at great risk, allowed for a successful assault by Australian special forces onto the compound where the rebels were hiding. That raid had prevented what was brewing to be a civil war in the fledgling small nation.

The plane shuddered as the rear wheels touched the tarmac, quickly followed by the front ones.

A textbook landing.

"Ladies and Gentlemen, welcome to Dili. Local time is three-thirty in the afternoon," announced the pilot as the plane slowed down and commenced taxiing towards the terminal.

Kryton closed his eyes for a moment, sighed and thought back to that night. Once the position of the rebel leader's location had been appropriately fixed in the highlands in the centre of the country, Kryton and his team called in the special forces assault force, who came flying in low on four blacked out Blackhawk helicopters under an hour later.

Kryton's two-man support team had acted as a sniper pair, observing the group of huts in the small village where the rebels were hiding and being prepared to give direct fire support to the assault team. Meanwhile, Kryton and the Timorese man, who was with the team to help identify the location of the rebels, took a position behind the snipers where Kryton maintained communications with the commander of the assault force, ultimately signalling the exact location of the small hut containing the rebel leader with an infrared laser targeting device.

The assault was by the book, with two of the helicopters offloading a platoon of commandos utilising fast rope as their insertion technique almost on top of the small village, while the other two helicopters landed in an elevated rice field nearby, their platoon of commandos pouring out and cutting off potential escape routes. Once all of the soldiers were off of the helicopters, the noisy aircraft had returned to the sky to provide additional overwatch and aerial fire support.

A short gunfight then ensued between the Australians and the rebels, resulting in three enemy KIA and the capture of the rebel leader, with no casualties in the assault force save for a fractured ankle sustained by a junior commando who had only recently received his sherwood green beret of the 2nd Commando Regiment.

The intelligence they had managed to obtain from that young Timorese man had endeared the lad to Kryton, but not nearly as much as what he did in the moments after the assault had finished.

While conducting an exfiltration away from the village and back to where they had cached their 'NGO' Toyota Landcruiser, Kryton's team stumbled upon three armed rebels who had been out of the village during the assault.

They essentially saw each other at the same time.

Kryton raised his M-4 shortened carbine, firing two shots and dropping the lead man instantly. The remaining two rebels managed to fire some bullets from their old .303 hunting rifles, injuring one of the support team before his partner managed to kill both of them with two rapid double taps from his own M-4.

Just as Kryton walked up to confirm his kill, a noise emanated from the darkened bushes to his left. Sensing the danger, the Timorese man jumped in front of Kryton, taking a bullet in his shoulder that would have otherwise mortally wounded the Australian. Kryton responded immediately, raising his weapon and unloading most of the magazine into the previously unseen rebel, an emotive reaction to seeing his friend hit by a bullet meant for him.

The team had then removed themselves from the engagement zone and conducted first aid on the Timorese man.

A brave young Timorese, codenamed *Pegasus*, who now needed Kryton's help.

A young man named Carlos.

5

The stifling heat hit Kryton as he descended the passenger stairs and walked onto the tarmac. It was a far cry from the colder temperatures that Canberra was experiencing at that time of year. He had come prepared, however, and the warm olive-green pullover that he had worn when leaving his home town now sat in his black backpack. He wore a charcoal grey polo shirt over full-length khaki pants. A pair of dark coloured Merrell lace-up shoes enclosed his feet.

Comfortable, but rugged enough to deal with most terrain.

It was what was known as the standard *operator* uniform; operator being a common term used to describe special forces soldiers, but often extended to include intelligence and paramilitary officers. It was also the clothing worn by spies, mercenaries and U.N. officials alike in third world countries.

He followed the other passengers across the tarmac and into the terminal. A local police officer stood by the entrance.

"Botarde," said Kryton, using the Tetum word for *good afternoon.*

The diminutive officer nodded, smiled and replied in the same manner, clearly intimidated by the size of the much stockier Australian, but appreciative of the respect shown to him when all of the other passengers had simply walked straight past without even so much as a nod.

Kryton only had his carry-on luggage. His brief from Jonas back in Canberra before he left was to make contact with Pegasus, elicit the information that he had and to return home.

ASIS would deal with whatever intelligence came from it – if any.

That suited Kryton just fine.

He was still jaded with how he had been treated by the army, and by extension, the Australian government. His injuries from the IED blast he was in during his last deployment to Afghanistan had healed, and in his mind, he was still fully fit to continue his duties.

The military doctor saw it differently. He saw a man with numerous injuries from years of intensive combat, parachuting, advanced hand-to-hand sparring, as well as the physically demanding suite of intensive special operations intelligence training, both in Australia and with the U.S. intelligence community.

In short, the doctor saw a medical basket case waiting to happen and decided to try to save the taxpayer from having to fund the inevitable medical bills that would follow.

'Not fit for deployment,' read the note at the top of Kryton's medical file.

He had been shattered.

He took the posting to RMC, but he couldn't envisage a future in the army teaching marksmanship full time to recruits, so he took his pension and thanks to a well-written letter to the Chief of Army from his Commanding Officer, had been allowed to stay as a reservist. This allowed him to be more selective about the type of work he wanted to do, such as instructing officer cadets in martial arts.

Jonas had attempted to get Kryton to follow him from the army into the service full time, not just as secondee on joint ASIS-military operations. However, the senior executives of the service, some who had never actually served in hostile parts of the world, only saw a broken soldier. They saw the future as being in the university graduates with coding skills, not in field experienced men in their late thirties.

The paramilitary skills the service leveraged off for the more dangerous tasks stayed with the special operations arm of the Australian Defence Force, and Kryton was no longer part of the regular ADF.

Kryton moved through immigration checks and towards the side of the terminal. He stood near a tourist information signboard. He smiled reminiscently at seeing some of the old towns and villages he once knew now advertised as tourist destinations. With its sparkling blue water and numerous reefs, Timor-Leste did, in fact, have some of the best SCUBA diving locations in the world, and almost half of the passengers on the plane had been young adults with large backpacks in one hand and *Lonely Planet* guidebooks in the other.

He turned to face the inside of the terminal, holding a copy of *The Australian* newspaper and leaning against the tourist sign.

'Chinese influence in South Pacific expanding,' read the headline.

Kryton was more interested in reading the horse racing news – his one vice. He flicked through the form guide for the upcoming weekend's races. He liked the look of a colt in the fifth in Adelaide, unimpressively named *Fat Possum*.

Hope he doesn't run like one, though, Kryton thought to himself with a chuckle.

A moment later, a well-built Caucasian man approached the signboard and looked at some of the advertisements. He had a rolled-up magazine in his hand, and wore a pair of aviator sunglasses, *Top Gun* style.

"The chicken is in the doghouse," the man said nonchalantly in an Australian accent, still looking at the sign board.

Kryton maintained his composure and kept reading his paper.

"I zed, zee chicken iz in zee dawghaus," said the man again, in a terrible attempt at a Russian accent, which actually sounded more Bavarian.

Kryton adjusted his position slightly, and a small grin appeared on his face. He looked up out of the corner of his eye. The appearance of the man looking at the signboard and pursing his lips making a fish face caused him to break his composure and start laughing out loud.

"Aww, c'mon mate, I was about to do the shoe phone routine," lamented the man to Kryton, as the two shook hands and embraced each other.

Kryton looked the man up and down with a big smile on his face.

Standing before him was Shane Cavan, simply known as Cav.

"How are you, mate?" said Kryton to his old friend.

In his late thirties, same as Kryton, they had joined the army together before they had both served as paratroopers. Cav then successfully endured the gruelling selection course for the 2nd Commando Regiment and was now on a rotation as a bodyguard conducting duties in the Personal Security Detachment – PSD – teams within the Regiment.

"They didn't tell me you'd be my support team," said Kryton as the two men walked through the terminal.

"We were passing back through Darwin after taking yet another politician on a photo op to the Middle East, and we got the call. We arrived late last night and chilled at the embassy. I was only briefed on who I would be babysitting this morning," Cav explained.

Kryton looked at Cav, unimpressed.

"Babysitting!? Thanks a lot," remarked Kryton, trying not to laugh.

"Who's your partner?" he asked Cav.

"An American, on exchange from the teams," said Cav, using the term used to refer to the U.S. Navy SEALs. "Nice guy, solid operator."

The two walked into the carpark and past the taxi lines. Several drivers petitioned their services to the two much larger men, but they respectfully declined.

A small motorised scooter brushed past them at speed as they walked towards the rear of the carpark, a teen and his companion without helmets thinking nothing of it. The two men just looked at each other.

"Good to be back," Kryton said sarcastically.

Cav smiled and nodded.

"So, what's with all the codenames and stuff?" Cav asked.

Kryton chuckled and rolled his eyes.

"It's not a requirement of our spymasters," Kryton said, shaking his head. "Someone was having you on."

Cav looked at Kryton, obviously feeling foolish. He appreciated a good gag, just not at his own expense.

The two men arrived at the side of a dirty white Landcruiser, reversed into a position in the carpark with its engine running – standard procedure for PSD teams, but in this case more about ensuring the internal air-conditioning remained cold. Cav jumped into the front passenger seat on the left while Kryton jumped into the back-passenger seat directly behind him.

The cool breeze of the air-conditioning was of great relief to him.

Sitting in the driver's seat was another solid man, wearing a trucker style black baseball cap and dark wraparound sunglasses.

"Clay Dalton – Zach Kryton," said Cav as he introduced his partner in the support team to his old friend.

"Call me CD," said Dalton in a distinct Texan drawl with a large, friendly smile, reaching over his shoulder and extending a hand to Kryton in the rear of the vehicle.

"Nice to meet you, mate," replied Kryton, noticing the firm grip on the American.

Why do SEALs always seem to be from Texas? he thought to himself.

Dalton released the handbrake and gently eased the Landcruiser forward and drove towards the entrance of the airport. The smell of aviation fuel was soon replaced by the mixture of humidity and burning rubbish as the trio drove into the side streets and towards the main Dili thoroughfare.

The stench immediately brought Kryton back to his early forays into the small nation as a young paratrooper. He asked Cav to turn up the air-conditioning.

"So," began Cav as he turned the dial to allow for increased airflow, "mind telling us what the hell we're doing here?"

6

The Landcruiser drove steadily east on President Nicolau Lobato Avenue, the main east-west thoroughfare in Dili. A myriad of scooters, small vans, other four-wheeled drives, as well as numerous pedestrians and dogs, filled the road. There were few traffic lights in Dili, and most drivers adhered closely to the principle of 'might is right'.

"What have they briefed you on?" Kryton asked the two operators sitting in the front.

"We were sitting in the airport in Darwin awaiting the flight back to Sydney when we were re-directed here. The Defence Attaché is an ex-operator but even he didn't have much of a clue, just that we needed to provide protection support for some spy," Cav informed Kryton.

"All good with me," added Dalton, "I've never been to Dili before," the Texan said enthusiastically.

Kryton immediately warmed to the American, a humble operator was a good operator in his experience.

"I'm afraid I can't elaborate too much either," said Kryton.

He moved his position in the vehicle so that he was sitting in the middle seat. He propped himself forward so that his two companions could hear him speak over the loud hum of the air-conditioner.

"Early yesterday morning there was an incident down at the harbour. A local man working as a security guard was killed and his partner ran off after being shot at," Kryton explained.

"That partner went straight to our embassy and used a codename that triggered the service to seek me out. He was a source I used to run here years ago."

"The service is what we call our foreign intelligence service, like your CIA," Cav explained to Dalton.

"I've heard of them," Dalton said.

"He's pretty shaken and apparently he's got some important information, but he won't talk to anyone but me, that's all I know," Kryton continued.

"So where is he now?" asked Dalton.

"The station members have him in their secure offices within the embassy," said Kryton, referring to the staff posted to the service's offices at the embassy, usually under the cover of political diplomats.

"We were in there earlier and didn't see him. Must have been hiding him! So, cops involved?" asked Dalton.

"Apparently not yet," replied Kryton, "the local news has reported a dead security guard and one guard missing, so their investigations are unaware of our interest and involvement. He's a pretty switched on sort of guy, so I can only assume it's something significant if he asked for me."

The Landcruiser maintained its easterly direction, crossing the Comoro River as it moved into the denser part of the capital. Kryton looked down as they crossed the bridge and watched as the local sand digging trucks started to move off of the dry river bed at the end of their day. Dark clouds began to gather, indicating that the afternoon storms were imminent.

"So, what's the plan?" Cav asked Kryton.

"Well, you blokes are here to look after me because it's standard procedure," said Kryton, patting his two colleagues on the shoulder sarcastically.

He knew they would have rather returned home after their Middle-East operation.

"Counterintelligence requirements?" asked Cav.

"No, this is a straight-up visit. No covers, no cloak and dagger. Well, apart from the pick-up at the airport," Kryton said laughing at his friend's expense. "But I'll be honest, it does sound like a lot of manpower to talk to one guy."

"So *why* did you come?" asked Dalton innocently as he maintained his eyes on the road.

Cav looked back at Kryton knowingly. He already knew the answer.

Kryton recited the story to Dalton about the night that Carlos saved his life.

"Jesus! He sounds like one tough kid," said Dalton genuinely impressed.

"Yeah, I like to think so," Kryton said.

"Anyway, we looked after his medical bills. It was only a flesh wound," Kryton continued, using the famous phrase from *Monty Python*.

They all laughed, the way that combat veterans do when discussing wounds and battle injuries that don't kill you. Dark humour was one form of stress relief, and Australian and American soldiers used it extensively.

"However, the poor kid wasn't allowed to join their army though after that, and he's maintained the cover story that he was shot in a hunting accident ever since. Besides, I owe him my life," Kryton said.

He paused for a moment and looked ahead into the distance, recalling to himself that night and how close he had come to being killed. The sound of Dalton sounding the horn to warn off an errant dog crossing the road brought him back into the present.

"So, that's why I am here, CD…and I'm afraid to say, you two as well!"

"Always here to serve you intelligence pests," joked Cav.

Cav had supported many intelligence operations and was grateful to be working with Kryton again. Although Kryton could easily have managed the task by himself, the service was funding it, and the protocol stated that a support team went too.

The trio pulled up to the front of a gated compound and stopped next to a small guardhouse. A Timorese security guard came out, a big smile on his face.

Dalton wound the window down.

"How y'all doing?" asked the large American, showing a small identification card.

Kryton and Cav also held up their military identification cards.

"Obrigadu, Maun," said the guard, thanking them respectfully in Portuguese.

The guard waved to his colleague in the guardhouse, and the large boom-gate opened up in front of their vehicle.

Multi-level, painted almost all white and heavily influenced by colonial Portuguese architecture, the Australian Embassy fitted in well with its surroundings, located near the heart of Dili.

Dalton drove down the side of the main building. Barbed wire adorned the top of the exterior wall, yet somehow it didn't detract from the overall aesthetics of the place. He pulled up next to a smaller, non-descript villa detached from the main embassy building.

It looked like a suite of accommodation buildings you might find at a tropical resort.

In actuality it was the ASIS station, Timor-Leste.

Kryton looked around. He noticed some of the changes they had made since he was last inside the compound. The in-ground pool was a particularly welcome addition, he thought.

He also noticed the lack of security guards armed to the teeth. The Australian government typically hired private contractors to guard their embassies in more hostile places, such as Baghdad. Most were ex-soldiers anyway, looking to ply their trade for a much larger paycheque than the army was offering. Dili was rated a low-security risk, so employing a few local guards promoted goodwill amongst the population.

The three men got out of the vehicle. The humidity hit Kryton once again.

A quick dip in that pool might help, he thought to himself.

7

Kryton looked around and observed the inside of the embassy compound. Rain began to lightly fall from the sky, and the faint sound of thunder could be heard in the distance. He watched as a ginger coloured cat scampered up a tree and over the wall.

"This way," said Cav as they walked towards the front door of the villa.

The three men passed through a wooden door and into a darkened foyer.

"Phones?" asked Cav, indicating that personal electronic devices needed to be kept outside and on the small table in the foyer.

Kryton had already removed his phone and proceeded to place it down on the table, where several others were already sitting.

He knew the drill.

Cav swiped a small card over an electronic keypad next to a thicker steel door and entered a code. A small beep accompanied by a green light opened it.

The three men entered the Secure Compartmented Information Facility – the SCIF. This security accredited building allowed for the discussion and transmission of top-secret communications and was where the spies ran their operations from.

A man wearing an Australian camouflage uniform was standing over a table centred in the middle of the room.

"Zach Kryton – Colonel Rob Oakover," said Cav introducing his friend to the Defence Attaché.

"Nice to meet you, Kryton, I've heard a lot about you," said the army officer as he extended his hand.

"Nice to meet you too, sir," replied Kryton respectfully as he returned the handshake. "All good things, I hope."

A tall and wiry man, the Defence Attaché had previously commanded a special forces unit back in Australia, and like many of his predecessors from those elite units, the army had big plans for him.

"Of course," laughed Oakover.

The four men gathered around the table.

"Well, I know you've had a long two days, so let's get down to it," commenced Oakover talking directly to Kryton.

Kryton nodded. He never liked wasting time, and he appreciated that the senior officer didn't waste it making unnecessary small talk or delivering lengthy platitudes.

"As you know, your man Carlos rocked up at the front gate of this embassy about dawn yesterday morning," began Oakover.

"He asked to speak to someone in the military, but since it was early none of my staff was in yet. The guards then placed him in the visitor waiting area."

"What happened then?" asked Kryton, sipping on a bottle of cold water that Dalton had just handed him.

"Well, it was lucky actually, the embassy staff were about to call the local police and turf him out when my assistant, Warrant Officer Phillips, arrived for work. The young lad ran up to him and asked for you personally and he used the codename *Pegasus*," Oakover continued.

"I arrived at work not long after. I spoke to Carlos and he said he couldn't talk to me. I tried to look up the codename in the systems with our counterparts here at the station, but we couldn't find anything that wasn't sealed and restricted. Their checks back to their headquarters in Australia immediately led back to you."

"I don't understand, why is that codename so secretive that it couldn't have been dealt with by someone here, I mean, aren't y'all spies anyway?" asked Dalton using typical military logic.

"Because Pegasus isn't just any source, is he Zach!" asked a female voice from the doorway leading to another office adjacent to the SCIF.

The four men turned to face her.

Standing before them was a slender young lady, early-thirties, wearing beige cargo pants and a pink blouse with the sleeves rolled up. Her auburn brown hair was tied back into a ponytail and a pair of Oakley sunglasses sat atop her head.

"No, he's not," replied Kryton, desperately trying to conceal the look of surprise on his face as he recognised the civilian head of the station.

"I take it you know our station chief," asked Oakover.

31

"You could say that," replied Kryton, trying to remain nonchalant.

"Nice to see you again, Zach," she said with a sly smile on her face as she joined them by the table.

"How are you, Jo?" Kryton replied.

Dalton looked at Cav seeking any explanation as to the connection, but Cav could only shrug his shoulders suggesting that he had no idea how they knew each other.

"What do you mean *not just any source*?" asked Oakover, seeking to bring them back onto topic.

"Carlos – codenamed Pegasus – was a *very* well-placed source," said Kryton. "His regular information was perfectly accurate, and we think it potentially stopped a civil war thanks to our assault on the rebels. He's the sort of source that you try to maintain a working relationship with using just one handler," he continued.

"And that was you?" asked Dalton.

Kryton nodded.

"So, when I returned home after things had quietened down here, we still wanted to be able to use him one day if needed. I taught him that if he ever became aware of anything significant that we might be able to use, to contact the embassy and use the codename Pegasus."

That was what he had told his superiors that he had said to Carlos, at least. In reality, Kryton had told Carlos that he owed him his life and that he would come if ever he needed help, and he was to use the codename to find him.

"Why did he work for us?" asked Oakover.

"Well, after INTERFET, much of the local population was eager to help us get the country back on the road to peace, but there were still many pro-Indonesian militias running about, so it was hard for them to do that openly. Some simply had better and more sensitive information than others, and we turned that into actionable intelligence by running them as confidential sources," explained Kryton.

"So how did he get *his* information?" asked Cav, starting to sense something significant.

Kryton looked at the group standing before him.

"Because his father was the former president, Jose Ramirez."

Cav's jaw dropped slightly before he mouthed a small *wow*.

"How come I wasn't told this?" asked Oakover curtly and visibly frustrated, like the way all army officers get when they feel they've been deprived of information.

"Because I didn't know either, until just now," said Jo calmly looking straight at Kryton. "I just spoke to Canberra and they told me that now that Zach is here, we could be fully briefed in. Our little station doesn't get to manage sources up at that level. Oh, by the way, Jonas says hi."

I bet he does, thought Kryton as he realised that his so-called friend had conveniently failed to tell him who the station chief was. Kryton didn't mull on that for too long; after all, he hadn't bothered to ask who the chief was.

"Who is President Jose Ramirez?" asked Dalton, the SEAL looking increasingly confused as to what the Australians were talking about.

"The now deceased Ramirez was the former vice-president, who ascended to the position of president when President Gusmano was almost killed in an assassination attempt by the rebels," Jo informed the American.

"Ramirez had the support of the army. He was a former guerrilla fighter during the Indonesian occupation," continued Kryton, "but after he came to power, he sacked half of the police force."

"So, Carlos isn't sure that he can trust the cops, in case they still hold grudges against his family?" asked Cav as he observed the pieces of the puzzle coming together.

Kryton nodded.

"Why did Ramirez sack them?" asked Dalton.

"Carlos and his family are *Loro'sae* – from the west of the country," said Kryton, "whereas most of the officers he sacked were from the east."

"What happened then?" enquired Dalton.

"Well, later that year, and about six months after our assault on the rebels, Ramirez was booted out of office at the election. Seems people didn't appreciate his sacking of half of the police force."

"Most of those officers got their jobs back later on though," Jo pointed out.

"But, they remembered," said Kryton, "so the Ramirez name isn't exactly popular among the police force."

"But once Carlos came here, why wouldn't he speak to one of the other embassy members?" asked Oakover. "I mean, I can understand his reluctance to go to the police, but he's worked with our army through you."

"Don't take it personally, sir," said Kryton, "if he's asked for me, I can only assume it's something significant – besides, I taught him the protocol. Army still gets to maintain the lead through my presence, even if I am now a reservist."

The Colonel nodded in approval. Army special forces and the national intelligence agencies had long maintained a working relationship based purely on both a mutual respect *and* distrust of one another. As a military intelligence professional, Kryton had been part of many operations that had come under the technical control of the service. However, he had still been a soldier, and would freely leverage the camouflage uniform to help him get army support when undertaking operations in support of the service.

Kryton didn't really care who took the lead. As far as he was concerned, he owed a debt to a young Timorese man and he had come to repay it.

"Okay, now that we all know the background, where's Carlos," asked Kryton impatiently.

Oakover looked over at Jo forebodingly.

"What?" asked Kryton, anticipating an answer he wasn't going to like.

"He left," said Jo calmly.

"He what?" said Kryton, clearly bemused.

Kryton was unhappy that he'd made the effort to come all this way and the reason for doing so wasn't presently available.

"We don't have the authority to keep him here, he's a Timorese citizen," said Jo.

Kryton looked over at his support team, but the confused look on their faces suggested that they hadn't been aware that Carlos was no longer at the embassy.

He looked at the roof.

Standard communication breakdown, he thought to himself.

"So, where is he?" Kryton asked authoritatively.

Experience told him that getting agitated never achieved results, so he would seek a solution rather than dwell on the problem.

Jo tried to stand up a little taller at her position by the table. It was obvious she didn't like being questioned by someone she considered subordinate.

Especially someone she had a history with.

"Jo is right, we couldn't keep him," interjected Oakover, looking to diffuse the tension. "But he did leave a note for you."

Oakover pulled a small handwritten note from an A4 binder he was holding and passed it to Kryton.

Kryton opened the folded piece of paper and looked at it closely.

A small smile appeared on his face.

Mister Zach, only you, find me at Vista – Target.

Kryton looked up at his team and nodded. He folded the piece of paper and placed it into his pocket.

"I know where he is. We're on."

The two men nodded back, then immediately moved outside the room and back to the vehicle to prepare for their next move.

Kryton then looked over to Oakover.

"Sir, we'll need low-signature kit, please. We're heading to the hills."

"You've got it," replied Oakover before leaving the room. He was impressed that Kryton was ready to take charge and get on with the job.

That was how the army did things.

"Wait, what are you doing?" asked Jo, clearly caught off guard by how quickly things now seemed to be happening.

Kryton moved around the table and stood next to her.

"He's gone to somewhere he feels safe. We'll just go up there and talk to him."

"Wait," said Jo, feeling intimidated and undermined, "this is still my operating area."

Kryton was ready to react assertively but instead took a moment to pause.

He took in a deep breath.

"Jo, I'm just here to talk to him, not take over your station. Jonas has authorised me free access to go wherever I need."

Jo looked back at him. Her face indicated she wasn't buying it.

He looked back at her with some empathy. It was hard being a woman working in a very alpha male environment, and he could only imagine that she had butted heads with Oakover a few times.

He leaned into the table to reduce his body profile – body language after all is ninety percent of communication.

"I'll keep you fully appraised, no cowboy stuff. You have my word," he said to her, an appeasing smile on his face.

She looked at him, trying to read his eyes.

His eyes eased their steely gaze, showing sincerity.

"This is the guy that saved my life."

"This is the –" she said in a shocked whisper before composing herself.

Jo knew the story, too.

She took a deep breath, broke eye contact with him and nodded.

"Okay. What do you need from me?"

Kryton stood up and turned around to face the table. A large map of Timor-Leste covered most of the surface. He pointed to a small town called Ermera, in the jungle hills about forty-five kilometres south-west of Dili.

"Here," said Kryton, "this is where we'll go. He has a family house here. I've spent time there before."

Jo nodded as she studied the map.

"The Colonel will sort us out with supplies, but what I need is a better idea of what happened at the harbour. Can we source that?" he asked her.

Jo looked at the map and pointed to the position that indicated Dili Harbour.

"There should be CCTV here we can try to access. Liaising with the police openly won't work as we have no genuine reason to know that information, so that might arouse suspicion."

"Can you find another way then?" Kryton asked her.

Jo looked at him and smiled.

"That's what we're trained for," she replied.

Kryton nodded in appreciation. He took a small notebook from his pocket and made some notes.

Oakover stuck his head around the door.

"Your team is all sorted," he said.

Kryton looked over at him and gave the thumbs up, his pen in his mouth as he fiddled around in his pockets with his other hand.

"Leave tomorrow?" asked the Colonel.

"No. We go tonight."

"Roger," he replied before leaving again, using the military term indicating he had heard and accepted Kryton's intentions.

Jo looked at him confused.

"It's going to be dark soon and it will take a few hours to get there," she said.

"And what do the Timorese do in the evening?" asked Kryton teasingly, as if the answer was obvious.

Jo smiled.

"They hang out with friends and family," she said as she remembered that locals took advantage of the cooler parts of the night to enjoy time outdoors at their homes or in their villages.

"Besides," he continued, "we need to know what's going on."

Kryton continued looking at the map and made some more notes. Even for what was expected to be a basic task, he still made time to plan properly. Jo walked towards the door to continue her own duties.

"Jo," he said, still looking down at the map.

The station chief stopped at the door and turned around.

Kryton looked up at her.

"Thanks – it's good to see you again, too."

She could sense the sincerity in his voice.

She nodded softly and looked at the ground. She looked back up at him, smiled and walked off.

8

The three men moved through the quietened streets on the outskirts of Dili, each now armed with a Glock-26 nine-millimetre pistol, neatly concealed in its holster in a place of preference on their hip pockets. Each man also carried two spare magazines.

They certainly didn't expect to need them.

Additionally, the team carried an encrypted satellite phone for communication back to the embassy.

They also carried their military identifications with them. The Australian Army still had a small presence in the country, mostly training staff helping to build and develop the fledgling Timor-Leste Army. They shouldn't be bothered by any police anyway – three white men in a Landcruiser was either foreign military or an NGO, and both were well respected and left alone by the locals.

It's not that they were expecting trouble, it was just that Carlos was holding what could potentially be sensitive information, and someone had already been murdered.

Something in Kryton's gut told him that whatever was going on, this was more than just a robbery gone wrong.

The street lights became less prevalent as they moved away from the suburbs and towards the foothills that surrounded the capital. Once they were out of the capital proper, Dalton applied the high beams of the Landcruiser to provide them with better visibility, and then he increased speed. Their only concerns on the road now would be wandering goats or cows, as well as the odd dog or chicken.

Kryton laughed.

"What is it?" asked Dalton.

"Just remembering all the dead dogs and chickens that we paid for over the years," said Kryton.

Cav laughed as well.

Dalton looked at them both, confused.

"In Australia, we have a general rule that you don't hit the brakes just because there is wildlife crossing your path, because it's unsafe to do so at the speeds we drive at on open roads," Kryton started telling the SEAL. "Unfortunately, in the early days of INTERFET and during the follow-on operations, some of our soldiers applied that rule when driving their Land Rovers through the streets. Problem was, the locals are mostly farmers and they let their animals roam freely, including on the streets," he continued.

"And?" Dalton asked inquisitively.

"Well, to keep good faith with the population, our headquarters started paying compensation to any locals who had an animal hit by one of our vehicles. It was good compensation too, well above what the animal was worth."

"Seems fair," said Dalton.

"Yeah, it was," added Cav, "however, after this policy became well known in the community, reports started coming in of locals literally standing by the side of the road and throwing animals in the path of our cars and trucks as they passed, then bringing that animal into our headquarters and claiming the compensation."

The three men started giggling.

"A mate in operations once told me that he saw the same dead dog presented three times for a payment," Kryton said, struggling to get the sentence out through his giggles.

That was the last straw. The three of them burst out laughing hysterically to the point Dalton almost ran off of the road.

They continued the drive into the darkened jungle. The roads were very well constructed, a legacy of the days of Indonesian occupation.

Kryton looked out of the window as they ascended the hills. Through the gaps in foliage on the side of the road, he could see back down to the lights of Dili. It had developed significantly since he had been there last. The provision of electricity to households had improved significantly, to the point that he could clearly see the shape of the coastline where the lights of the town stopped and the darkness of the open ocean began.

"So, how do you know he'll be there?" asked Cav.

Kryton reached into his pocket and took out the folded piece of paper Oakover had handed to him back at the embassy. He passed it to Cav.

Cav held it next to the glow of the LCD clock embedded in the dashboard. He read it out for Dalton's awareness.

"Explain," Cav said handing it back to Kryton.

"*Vista* is the name of Carlos' family's old estate up on the outskirts of Ermera. I spent more than a few nights there when I was working with him."

"What about *Target?*" asked Dalton.

Kryton chuckled.

"After he jumped in front of a bullet for me, it was only natural that he be given a nickname worthy of such an effort, don't you agree?" Kryton said to them both.

Cav and Dalton laughed together, appreciating the typically dark humour.

"And, what about the girl at the station, what's her story?" Cav asked mischievously, changing topic slightly, "or more to the point, what's your story?"

"Notice that, did you?" said Kryton, stating the obvious.

Cav reached up to the roof of the vehicle and flicked the internal light on. He lowered the front passenger seat sun visor, and using the mirror inside it he looked back at his friend in the rear seat. He lowered his head slightly and raised his eyebrows, indicating that he wanted to hear the story.

Kryton reached up and turned the light back off.

"Careful, you'll blind our poor Texan friend here."

"No worries," said Dalton, appropriately using an Australian idiom. "Spill it!"

Kryton sighed. For a moment he wondered whether he was sitting with two highly trained special forces operators, or in a high school locker room.

"Nothing special there, boys," Kryton said, trying to reduce their interest in his personal life. He knew they wouldn't give up, though.

"Jo was working as a junior analyst back in Canberra when I first went to work for the service. We went out a few times, and things started getting cosy," he told them.

"And?" asked Cav.

Kryton continued to look out of the window.

"Well, once I had finished my super spy training," he said sarcastically, "I started travelling a lot with work. She wanted more – I didn't. Simple as that."

"Really?" asked Dalton, seemingly not convinced.

Kryton shrugged his shoulders.

"I guess I just didn't think doing the type of work we do was conducive to a good relationship," he said.

The two men in the front nodded. They understood full well the toll that military life could take on relationships, and especially on those who worked in special operations. They had all been to one too many funerals of colleagues killed in the line of duty, and had experienced the heartbreaking scene of a grieving widow sobbing over the coffin of her beloved.

"Anyway, I broke it off. I'm not sure she's forgiven me yet."

"I don't know," said Cav, "she didn't appear too jaded."

Kryton knew that she wasn't. She wasn't that type of girl. She didn't hold grudges. They had had some great times together, but his work had been his priority.

His sole focus.

Until it was taken away from him.

"She's done well for herself, at least," mused Kryton.

The Landcruiser continued its journey.

A little under two hours later, they had passed through the township of Gleno.

Soon after, they entered Ermera. A small town, it served the farming families that resided in the hills and valleys surrounding it. Many locals walked for hours each day to shop at the markets.

Kryton lowered the window slightly.

They moved up the main street, a bumpy road carved into the countryside that was once sealed but which had fallen into disrepair in the years following INTERFET.

A beautiful all-white church took pride of place at the end of the street, with two large lights beaming upwards and illuminating its spire. Although night time, people were still out and about moving between shops and houses, just as Kryton had expected. The odd television could be seen on a front porch. Most of the shops and houses only had old-style globe bulbs for illumination, powered by the large diesel generator at the other end of the street.

"Where now?" asked Dalton.

"Go through that intersection and turn right," said Kryton as he pointed up ahead.

Their destination was two kilometres out of Ermera, along a makeshift road that although bumpy and rugged, would pose no problem for their Landcruiser.

They drove along the road at a slow pace. There were no lights outside of the main street and the road ran along a ridgeline. Any mistake in driving could prove fatal, as the steep hills plunged quickly into the valleys below.

Ten minutes later they arrived at the driveway of an old Portuguese style house, set back from the road.

There were no obvious lights on.

"Is this the place?" asked Dalton.

"It is," replied Kryton, trying to glance through the windscreen.

Dalton moved the Landcruiser slowly forward up the driveway, which was about one-hundred metres from the front of the house.

He stopped the vehicle about fifteen metres from the front door.

"I'll go and have a look," said Kryton.

He opened the door of the Landcruiser, stepped out and closed it behind him.

That's much nicer, he thought as the cooler air of the evening swept over him, a far cry from the humid air that had greeted him at the airport six hours earlier.

He couldn't see any obvious signs of movement or life.

He placed his hand over his right hip pocket to confirm the presence of the Glock.

It was habit.

He slowly approached the front of the house.

It was a path he had travelled on before during his previous visits to the sprawling estate, but the current lack of human activity was still unnerving.

Kryton stuck his hand out by his side and waved it slowly, indicating for Dalton to turn the lights of the vehicle up to a higher beam. This allowed him to better see the sides of the building by reducing the shadows created by the lower light.

He moved up onto the front step of the house and took the three steps up onto the front porch in slow succession.

He approached the large wooden front door and peered into the window that sat at waist height next to it.

Cav exited the car and joined Kryton by the door.

"Anything?" whispered Cav.

"Doesn't look like it," replied Kryton.

The two men stood on the front porch and looked at each other.

Kryton suddenly flared his nostrils and his face scrunched up.

"Do you smell that?" he asked Cav.

Cav stepped closer to Kryton and inhaled deeply.

"Oh, yeah now I can. What is it?" asked Cav.

"That smell – hot fish curry," Kryton told him, "and it tastes amazing!"

Kryton smiled, walked over to the door and knocked on it loudly three times.

"Carlos, get out here. I haven't come all this way to stand in the dark."

The two men stood there as some muffled speech emanated from inside the building.

A baby's loud crying voice quickly followed.

The sound of a bolt being unlocked came from behind the door, followed by the screeching sounds of a rusted door handle turning.

The door opened just slightly, and a Timorese face peered out and looked up at the two large Australians standing before him.

"Mister Zach!" exclaimed a beaming white smile.

It was Carlos.

He opened the door fully and stepped out towards Kryton. The two embraced like brothers.

"Hello mate, so good to see you," Kryton said as he gripped Carlos by the arms and looked down at him, smiling and giving him the once over.

It was a rough grasp, but one of affection and concern.

"Oh, Mister Zach, we didn't know it was you, I was worried it would be the police," Carlos said, his voice starting to tremble.

Carlos still called Kryton by the title *Mister* despite Kryton having told him numerous times to simply call him by his first name.

That's just how the Timorese did things. Very polite and respectful.

"It's okay, I'm here now," Kryton reassured him.

It was obvious that Carlos had heard the Landcruiser come up the driveway and had become frightened enough to turn all the lights off and hide.

Carlos composed himself and looked at Cav curiously.

"Carlos – meet Cav," Kryton said. "It's good, he's one of my guys."

Carlos grasped Cav's hand and shook it with both of his own. A sign of respect and warmth.

Kryton waved over to Dalton, who brought the Landcruiser up alongside the house. He turned the motor off and joined the two Australians on the porch.

Kryton introduced Dalton to Carlos. The little Timorese man's eyes widened as the large Texan grabbed him by the hand and shook it furiously.

"Hey little buddy, great to me ya," said the American with exuberant friendliness.

Carlos looked at Kryton with a nervous smile, almost pleading for help.

"Okay, let's not break him just as we get here," said Kryton jokingly as he placed his hand on Dalton's shoulder to reduce the intensity of his handshake.

Dalton realised he might have been a bit firm, and released the poor lad from his grasp.

"I'll go and call in our arrival," he said sheepishly, smiling at Carlos to show that he meant no harm.

Dalton and Cav moved back down to the vehicle to make contact with the embassy and let them know that they had arrived safely.

Although the drive to Ermera to meet with Carlos was expected to be a simple task, military planning still dictated timely communication with the operating base, which in this instance was the ASIS station back in Dili.

Carlos grasped his hand and rubbed it.

"Support team?" he asked Kryton.

"Support team," replied Kryton, impressed that Carlos remembered the old drills.

"Was I right to bring them?" he asked, transitioning from pleasantries to business.

"Oh, and Carlos," continued Kryton, "what did you mean *we?*"

Carlos looked up at his friend and the large beaming smile returned to his face.

"Come inside. I'll show you."

9

Carlos escorted Kryton into the foyer of the house and switched on the light. The interior was a mixture of classical Portuguese style with obvious local additions, such as woven tais – colourful locally made cloths – strewn over furniture and adorning the floors and walls.

"Ana," Carlos said calling out to an unseen figure.

A young lady holding a small baby emerged from behind a doorway that appeared to lead to the living room. She appeared nervous and wary of the Australian now standing in her house.

"Come, come," gestured Carlos to Kryton as he walked over to his wife and young baby.

Carlos spoke a few inaudible words of Tetum to the girl.

She looked up at Kryton, took a deep breath and smiled. She appeared more at ease once her husband had told her who Kryton was, yet she still remained nervous.

"Hello Ana, I'm Zach," the Australian said.

"We thought you might be the police coming to blame Carlos for what happened," she said softly.

Carlos had obviously informed her of what had happened at the harbour, and now Kryton knew for sure that Carlos didn't trust the local constabulary.

"I'm here to make sure you're all okay," Kryton reassured her.

She looked at him closely, and in an instant, she appeared more relaxed.

"Oh, Mister Zach, you're welcome here. Come in, come in," said Ana.

"Please, sit down," she said to him, motioning to a dining table.

"When did you get married?" asked Kryton, looking at Carlos with an expression of surprise.

"A few years ago, not long after my father died," Carlos told him.

Kryton placed a sympathetic hand on Carlos' shoulder. He knew that Carlos and his father weren't close, but simply being his father's son had meant that Carlos had endured his fair share of ridicule and abuse over the years from people who resented the former president.

Kryton really thought of Carlos as being like a little brother.

"And who is this young one?" asked Kryton as he and Carlos walked over next to Ana and looked down at the small child she held in her arms.

"This is my son, Juan Zachary," Carlos told him proudly.

Kryton looked at Carlos, somewhat confused.

"Zachary?"

"Yes, we named him after a good friend," Carlos said to Kryton.

Kryton was speechless.

Ana and Carlos looked at each other and smiled.

"Well, he's a smart kid, obviously!" Kryton told the proud parents.

"Mister Zach, Carlos has told me so much about when you worked together doing your medical work," Ana said to Kryton.

Kryton looked at Carlos knowingly. When the Australian had left Timor-Leste at the end of the assault on the rebel camp, he had told the young man that he would never be able to share the true nature of their working relationship with anyone, not even a future wife.

It was for his own safety.

It was also so that the service could leverage him again one day if they ever needed to, just in case Carlos decided to follow his father into politics and ascended to a lofty position with influence and access.

That's the thing about intelligence agencies – they think long term.

"He was a great help to us, a really good person," Kryton told her, heaping praise on the young man.

You don't know just how good, he thought to himself.

"We good to come in?" came an American voice from the front door.

Cav and Dalton were poking their head around the corner from the outside.

"Yeah boys, come on in," Kryton said to them.

He made the necessary introductions. The two men were impressed that Kryton now had a namesake.

"He's already better looking than you," whispered Cav jokingly in Kryton's ear as they all moved to sit around the dining table.

Kryton just shook his head and rolled his eyes.

"Ana, if I'm not mistaken, I smelt *Ikan Manas* when I first got here," said Kryton, using the Tetum words for hot fish curry.

Ana smiled, clearly impressed with Kryton's keen sense of smell.

"Yes, we have lots, too," she said. "I'll put Juan down to sleep again and we can eat."

"Ana, if you could please host our guests, I need to speak to Mister Zach," Carlos said to his wife.

She nodded and moved into another room to try to get her son back off to sleep.

"I'll be outside, eat up. But save some for me," Kryton told his support team as the two men made themselves comfortable at the table.

They were both hungry and would eat anything at that point.

Carlos took Kryton out through the house and onto the back porch.

The night sky was littered with stars, peering through the few clouds that remained from the afternoon storm. The noise of crickets and bats provided ambience, and Kryton remembered fonder times when he and Carlos sat drinking whiskey and sharing life stories, looking down into the valleys below at sunset.

The view was always impressive.

"Okay mate, I've come a long way," Kryton commenced. "How can I help?"

"Thank-you, thank-you for coming Mister Zach, I'm so very sorry you had –" Carlos said before having to compose himself.

He was almost weeping at this point.

He had obviously done his best to look stoic for his wife, but Kryton could clearly see he was shaken. That was unusual for Carlos

"It's fine, mate. I said I'd always be there for you. It's not a problem. You're okay."

Kryton had always been impressed about how genuine and humble Carlos had been, but this vulnerability was a new side of a person he had only ever seen full of bravado.

He placed his hand on Carlos' arm to help calm him.

"We all get shaken, so whatever is going on we'll deal with together, like we always used to," Kryton said.

Carlos calmed down enough to begin to tell Kryton what happened.

He recited how he had sent young Alberto out to do the rounds of the wharf in the rain, and that he decided to go after him to give him the umbrella.

He told him how he saw three Chinese men before one shot Alberto at close range.

He then told Kryton of the sheer terror he felt as two of the men chased him into the warehouse, where he hid, willing his heart to not beat so loud as he feared his pursuers would be able to find him because of it.

He told Kryton how he had hitched rides all the way back to his family estate and had been too scared to talk to the police, and didn't know if he could trust the Australians at the embassy.

Kryton listened intensely to every detail.

Carlos told Kryton about the two long, military-style boxes that he had seen on the back of the truck. In their rush, the Chinese men had failed to secure the green canopy, and the rear of the truck had been exposed with the wind.

"How do you know they were military boxes?" asked Kryton.

"We get arms shipments monthly from Europe and America through the warehouse," Carlos informed him. "They have heavy-set wooden boxes that look similar to those I saw."

"Were you expecting any that night?" Kryton asked.

"No, there were no deliveries due that night at all, they had all been cancelled. Nothing was due to come alongside the wharf."

"Cancelled? By whom?" Kryton asked.

"The Harbour Master. He told me as I started the shift."

Kryton thought for a moment.

"When is your next shift supposed to be?" he asked Carlos.

"Not for a few days. I work for five days on and then get three days off. I stay at the warehouse during my work week then come back here for my time off."

Kryton considered the optics of the situation. So far, any detective worth their salt would suspect Carlos, as he had technically gone missing from a crime scene. That was an issue they would have to deal with later.

"Were there any distinguishing features? Any markings on the boxes?" he asked Carlos.

"I couldn't see much because of the rain," Carlos told him. "However, I saw a few numbers, stencilled on the side."

"Do you remember what they were?" asked Kryton.

"Yes – one, seven, eight, five. That was on one of the boxes. I couldn't see the other."

"That's okay, you were very smart to notice that. Well done!"

Carlos wasn't a trained soldier. He had already given so much for Kryton, and now he had just witnessed his friend get murdered. Kryton felt that boosting the young man's self-esteem with some genuine compliments seemed the least that he could do.

Kryton looked through the window into where the others were sitting. Dalton was engaged in an animated conversation with Cav, with Ana looking bemused and horrified at the same time.

"How much does Ana know?" he asked Carlos.

"She knows why I haven't told the police, and she understands it's because of my father," Carlos replied. "She only knows you as an aid worker."

Kryton nodded.

"I'm sorry about your friend at the wharf."

Carlos looked down at his feet, clearly still upset. He shrugged his shoulders.

"Perhaps I should have done more," he said.

"No – if you had you wouldn't be here now. It was a situation you had no control over," Kryton said to him.

Kryton looked back into the window and managed to get the attention of Cav. He placed his hand on his head with the palm face down – the hand signal Australian soldiers use in the field to discreetly say to another soldier *come over here to me*.

Cav nodded in acknowledgement.

He looked back at Carlos.

"Your focus now is your family, mate. They will be safe here. Go inside and look after Ana, and reassure her things will be okay. We'll help deal with the police."

Carlos looked up at Kryton and smiled. The presence of the Australian and his friends was comforting, and he felt much safer now. He walked back through the door and into the house.

Kryton turned to face back down into the darkened valley. A few scattered lights were the only visual indication that people were living down there.

Cav and Dalton joined him.

"Well?" asked Dalton.

Kryton turned to face his team and leaned against the small brick wall that was the ledge of the back porch.

He sighed.

"Well, something's going on," he started before fully briefing them on what Carlos had said.

Both of the support team operators thought for a moment.

49

"So, we've got three Chinese guys, a dead Timorese kid and possibly some weapons being smuggled into the country. Does that about sum it up?" asked Dalton.

Kryton nodded.

"So, let's just pass this to the local authorities," Dalton said.

"Can't, CD," sighed Cav knowingly.

"Why? Seems straight forward enough," responded Dalton logically.

"If it was just the murder, we'd probably be able to," Kryton told the American, "but the potential weapons smuggling makes it an issue for us."

"Us?"

"Australia," said Cav, looking at the American and winking with national pride.

"Two of our main national intelligence priorities are regional arms proliferation, and Chinese influence," Kryton told the Texan. "This is a red flag for us."

Dalton nodded that he understood.

"For us in the U.S. too, I would imagine," he stated.

"What sort of kit gets transported in long, wooden boxes?" Kryton asked rhetorically.

"Big kit," mused Cav.

"It sounds deliberately tactical," said Dalton looking at Kryton.

"How?"

"Well, it was done in the middle of the night. There were *only* two boxes. And these guys were willing to kill for it. If you want to smuggle arms generally, there are many other ways to do it – less risky, less violent. This was very specific."

Kryton looked up at Cav, who nodded in agreement with Dalton.

"I'll call this in," Kryton said, before moving off to the side of the house where the vehicle was parked.

He picked up the encrypted phone and fiddled with the buttons.

A click came across the earpiece followed by a dial tone.

It rang three times before a female voice answered.

It was Jo.

"Zach?" she asked.

"Yeah, Jo."

"How are you guys going up there?" she asked.

"We've made contact with Carlos. He's fine. But we might have something going on here."

50

Kryton proceeded to explain the situation to Jo, who listened intensely and asked a few clarifying questions, the way analysts do when looking to build an intelligence picture.

She's still a professional analyst at heart, Kryton thought to himself.

"Kryton, It's the DA."

Kryton's thought process was interrupted by the voice of the Defence Attaché who announced himself over the phone. Jo had obviously placed it onto speaker mode.

"Did you hear all that?" Kryton asked him.

"Yes. I'll speak to JOC and try to get some traction on the boxes," said the Colonel, referring to the Joint Operations Command, the three-star officer led unit that ran all ADF operations overseas.

"Roger," replied Kryton. "Also, ask about any unusual Chinese military activity in the area."

"You suspect something?" asked the Colonel.

"Hmm, just a hunch."

"Okay, I'll ask," he said to Kryton.

"Alright Zach, I'll brief Canberra. We'll keep this to ourselves at the moment, so we won't inform local authorities yet," said Jo.

"Good."

"You want to keep the lead on this?" asked Jo.

Kryton thought to himself. He didn't want to appear too eager. He had been left out of the game, and now this was a chance to play again, even if it was in something relatively low level.

"Sure," he responded, as nonchalantly as he could.

"Anything else?" she asked him.

"Yeah, work hard on that CCTV, it might be the only thing that clears Carlos from suspicion by the police. It will help us, too."

"Okay. I'll brief the Americans as well, they might be interested," Jo said. "What will you do now?"

"We'll rest here for a bit and then head back into Dili," said Kryton as he started making his way back towards the house.

"There's a Harbour Master I need to speak to."

10

The rising sun appeared through the canopy of the jungle, scattering light onto the road as the four men drove along the countryside, heading back towards Dili. After spending the night at Carlos' family estate to rest, they had returned to the Landcruiser to continue seeking answers.

Carlos had agreed to come with them to act as an interpreter, as well as to provide direction to the house of the Harbour Master, his superior at work.

Quietly, after several years of working a low-key job as a security guard, he felt a sense of excitement at helping Kryton again.

Being part of a team.

Feeling important.

The feeling he had hoped to find in the army, which was dashed because of his injury.

He sat in the back seat, next to Cav who was softly snoring in the seat next to him. Cav had undertaken the night watch and was now taking his turn to get some rest.

Kryton looked in the rear-view mirror from his position in the front passenger seat and observed Carlos rub his shoulder.

"How is it?" he asked.

"It's okay," replied Carlos, "holding the baby hurts it sometimes."

"A good problem to have," commented Kryton.

Carlos smiled. Family was everything in Timorese culture, and Kryton had listened to Carlos spend many a conversation discussing how he wanted to be a father one day.

For now, Carlos leaned up against the door and shut his eyes to get some rest. He was tired from having stayed up most of the night keeping Cav company and talking about soccer.

Dalton drove the vehicle through Gleno, already bustling as people headed towards the markets.

"How long have you got left on exchange?" asked Kryton, seeking to learn more about the American and to fill the drive with meaningful conversation.

"Six months," he replied. "Then I'll take some time off and head off on a bit of a vacation around the country."

"Anywhere in particular?"

"Kakadu, and Barossa Valley," said the SEAL.

Kryton looked at him bemused. They were very specific yet very contrasting locations. Dalton could tell that he should probably elaborate.

"Well, I watched *Crocodile Dundee*, and always wanted to see the outback of Kakadu," Dalton started.

"A completely accurate reflection of Australia," said Kryton sarcastically, as it seemed that most Americans judged his country on the famous movie, "although it is nice up there. And the Barossa Valley?"

"My family runs wineries in Texas, near Austin," Dalton said, "so I'm really into wines. I thought I might take the chance to do some study of your best wineries."

Kryton smiled and told Dalton about how he had grown up close to the winery district of the Barossa Valley not far from Adelaide, the capital of the state of South Australia.

"I'll head back and take over the business from my father once I'm finished with the navy," Dalton told him.

"All of your family in Texas?" Kryton asked.

"Just my folks, and my younger brother who is a doctor. He was really good at college ball but didn't make the NFL, so he focused on medicine instead. He lives in Houston with his wife and two daughters."

"So, no attachments?" probed Kryton.

"Just the navy," he said, "but I've still got a few months left down under," he added, looking at Kryton and winking.

Kryton laughed. A brother who is a doctor, a family that runs wineries. Wine*ries* – plural. It was obvious that Dalton came from a well to do family.

"So, why the navy?"

Dalton shifted position in his seat.

"Well, I came home from a night shift at the bottle boxing factory one morning, a job my father made us both do to learn and appreciate the business. It sucked."

Kryton laughed.

"My formative employment was at a service station doing the graveyard shift, so I get it," said the Australian.

"Anyway, I turned the television on and saw two buildings burning in New York City. I enlisted the following week and was at boot camp a few months later."

Kryton looked empathetically at Dalton. He always respected most of the U.S. servicemen and women he had met and worked with, and he appreciated the reasons why they had enlisted after the attacks on American soil that September morning. For most of them, the military wasn't about a paycheque. It was about something deep and personal.

"I spent nearly two years in the surface fleet but got sick of sitting over a weapons console. So, I applied to BUD/S and went off to Coronado," Dalton said, referring to the infamously gruelling U.S. Navy special warfare qualification pipeline – Basic Underwater Demolition / SEAL training.

"Fair enough!"

Kryton was really warming to Dalton and was glad to have him on the team.

Their vehicle continued along the winding roads, and after a while they were close enough to the edge of Dili to be able to look down across the sprawling semi-urban city from the top of the foothills. The cool of the evening was being rapidly replaced by the increased humidity the sun brought through its ascension into the sky.

The two men in the back stirred as the noise of car horns and general traffic increased as they got closer to the outer part of the city.

As they approached the city limits, Dalton asked where he should go to now.

"Carlos?" asked Kryton.

"Near the cathedral, behind the girl's school," Carlos replied.

Kryton gave the thumbs up, then pointed through the front windscreen to provide Dalton directions.

11

Dalton slowly manoeuvred the Landcruiser through the narrow residential streets of inner Dili. People on scooters, driving other cars and pushing carts all bustled for space. What looked like chaos was actually an efficient and well-managed process, where people were patient enough to take their turn to guide their respective modes of transport through the limited space available.

Everyone still got to where they needed to go.

The inner parts of Dili, away from the main thoroughfares, was an eclectic mix of villa-style houses, apartment-style complexes, corrugated iron shacks and the odd U.N. issued tent. Nearly twenty years after INTERFET, the city that had been destroyed by rampaging militias was showing signs of investment and growth, though the remnants of that destruction were still visible.

"Up ahead, on the left," said Carlos, reaching through the front seats with his hand and pointing to a double story yellow building on the left-hand side of the road.

Dalton eased the Landcruiser to the side of the road as far as he could, seeking to avoid blocking the entire street. The large vehicle wasn't exactly suited to streets designed for motorcycles, pushcarts, and sedans.

"Guess we'll go and have a look," Kryton said as he pulled out a small radio communication set from the kit bag Oakover had provided back at the embassy. He placed the earpiece into his left ear and manipulated the plastic wire cord down through his polo shirt, ensuring the mouthpiece was to the front of his body, concealed under his shirt. He connected the metal jack into the small receiver on his left hip pocket.

Standard issue PSD communications kit.

He pressed the button on the receiver.

"CD, you got me?" he said quietly into the mouthpiece.

The small handheld radio Dalton had pulled from the same bag squawked to life, so Dalton fiddled with the volume buttons to lower the noise.

"L and C," replied the American into his radio, using the abbreviated term for *Loud and Clear*.

They had tested the radios before they left the embassy, but it was good practice to confirm operability if they hadn't been used for a while.

It was a mantra special operation forces the world over lived by – *always test your kit*.

Kryton gave the thumbs up and got out of the vehicle with Carlos.

He looked back through the lowered front passenger window to speak to his team.

"Cav, you contact Jo and let her know we've made it to the Harbour Master's place. CD, if you get pressure from the locals for this beast being parked here, start to do laps around the block and I'll grab you on the way out."

Both men nodded, and Kryton turned to join Carlos.

They started walking up an inclined driveway into what looked like a small double story apartment complex.

Pretty modern, for Dili at least, Kryton thought to himself.

They walked around the corner of the edge of the building, which was essentially a U-shaped complex, the hollow part being a sort of carpark.

It seemed quiet. Most of the residents would already be out for the day.

A few stray dogs ran past as they began to ascend a set of metal stairs up to the first level. Kryton walked just behind Carlos under the awning and along the balcony, letting him lead the way.

"So, what's this guy's name anyway?" Kryton asked Carlos.

"Antonio," replied Carlos.

"And he should be home?"

"Yes, he decided to take a few days off."

A Harbour Master deliberately absent from work after an arms smuggling incident had occurred, who also cancelled other deliveries on the night it happened. There were starting to be a few red flags that were now of interest to Kryton.

Carlos stopped in his tracks, so quickly that Kryton bumped into the back of him.

Carlos pointed to a red plywood door in the corner of the complex, a few metres from where the two men stood. The door handle had been broken off and the area around where the lock would be had obviously been damaged. The door was slightly ajar, and a small floor mat that sat out the front was askew.

Kryton looked around, looking for anyone else present.

"We're at the front of his apartment, it looks like it's been robbed. I'm going in for a look," Kryton said calmly into his radio.

"Copy that," came the reply into his earpiece from Dalton.

"Wait here," Kryton said to Carlos, now taking a serious tone.

Something didn't feel right.

He pulled the Glock from its holster and held it by his side.

He would only use it as a last resort in self-defence, but even up until that point it still made for a great intimidation tool.

Kryton prodded the door open with his foot to look inside. It looked like a rather large apartment, especially by Timorese standards. He noticed that a small coffee table had been kicked over, and there was some newspapers strewn across the floor.

He pressed the button on his radio.

"Cav, join me mate," he said.

"Roger. Coming," came the reply through the earpiece.

He looked across at Carlos and placed his palm up, indicating the young man should stay where he was.

Kryton moved through the door slowly and quietly. His pistol grasped in both hands in front of him at forty-five degrees – known as the *ready* position.

He took a few steps before he heard a groaning noise on the ground coming from around the corner to his left. He moved towards the edge of the living room which appeared to lead to a hallway.

As he came around the corner, he looked down and saw a Timorese man huddled up in a sitting position against the wall.

A pool of blood surrounded him, and he clutched at his stomach.

Kryton made eye contact with the man, who raised his free arm towards Kryton, pleading for help. The man then looked slightly to his left and over Kryton's shoulder. They widened just enough for Kryton to gather that something was behind him.

He rapidly pivoted on the spot and went straight down onto his right knee.

He raised his pistol just as the whizzing sound of a bullet went hurtling over his head.

If he'd been any slower, the bullet would have gone right between his eyes.

The spectacularly fast move by Kryton had been accompanied by his removal of the safety on his pistol. By the time he had taken a firing position, he was ready to engage a target.

The figure of a man filled his sight.

He instinctively fired two bullets aimed at the direction of where the shot had come from.

The double-tap – the standard drill for engaging a target and designed to at least make an assailant put their head down, ostensibly giving the firer just enough time to fire a third, more accurate shot if needed.

His first two shots slammed into a cupboard that sat on the wall of the kitchen that was next to the living room.

Wood shards went flying, forcing a Chinese man holding a pistol to hug the wall adjacent to the cupboard in an attempt to take cover.

The man quickly leaned back out into the open, his pistol raised and looking to actually hit his target this time.

The view was minimal, but it was enough for Kryton to get his third shot off just as the upper half of the Chinese man's body came into view.

This time his shot was more accurate, and it glanced off of the right shoulder of the Chinese man's outstretched arm. The man quickly hugged the wall again, just as Cav came flying through the front door, his own pistol held in the hands of his extended arms.

He had obviously heard the start of the firefight.

I'm rusty, Kryton managed to think to himself despite all that was happening.

Cav quickly scanned the room, his eyes and the sight of his pistol lined up, ready to engage any threat.

He noticed Kryton on his knee, pointing his own weapon at the entrance to the kitchen, still aiming at where the Chinese man had appeared a moment earlier.

Cav took a step forward, and then also noticed the Timorese man propped up against the wall.

Kryton looked back at Cav and mouthed the words *one tango,* indicating a hostile enemy.

Cav nodded in acknowledgement.

A muffled sound came from the kitchen, and then footsteps of someone hurriedly running the other way from where the Australians now were.

Kryton jumped to his feet, his pistol still firmly pointed at the kitchen.

Carlos suddenly appeared at the door.

Kryton looked over at him. He was furious and impressed at the same time.

He was furious that Carlos had come unarmed into a room that had just had bullets flying through it. The last thing he wanted was for the young man to take another bullet because of him.

But he was impressed because he knew that Carlos wanted to know that his Australian friend was okay, and would risk his own life, again, to ensure that he was.

"Stay there," he said to Carlos firmly.

They heard the noise of smashing glass come from down the hallway where the Chinese man had run off to.

Kryton moved forward slowly and deliberately, Cav behind his shoulder, both of them now in a two-man assault formation and ready to conduct room combat, a skill they had perfected through multiple deployments to Afghanistan.

They entered the room where the smashing glass had come from, just in time to see a body jump from the ledge.

A trail of blood was scattered on the floor.

Kryton and Cav ran towards the window where the Chinese man had jumped from and looked down through the shattered glass to see him land on the tiled roof of the small villa next door.

The man stood up, grasping his right shoulder with his left hand whilst still holding his pistol.

"CD, medical kit, now – we're in contact," Kryton said into his radio to the SEAL in the Landcruiser.

"We go?" asked Cav, eager to get through the window and after the injured Chinese man who was limping across the roof.

"Just me, I need you on the wounded guy, we need him. Get Carlos to fetch the medical kit from Dalton."

Cav had a reputation as an excellent combat medic. He had only recently returned from mentoring operations in Iraq, where Australian and U.S. special forces had advised their Iraqi counterparts on the front line during their fight against ISIS. He had saved numerous Iraqi lives during that operation and had been recommended for a medal.

59

"Roger," said Cav, as Kryton hauled himself through the window, preparing to jump in pursuit of the Chinese man.

He jumped the few metres down onto the tiled roof. His knees buckled slightly as he landed, so he tucked his body up and performed a forward roll to slow the momentum of the fall.

The move would have impressed any parkour enthusiast.

He stood up and started to follow the blood trail.

"CD, in pursuit of one tango, on foot moving west parallel to the road. Chinese guy with a wound to the right shoulder. He's still armed," Kryton said into the radio, giving the details to Dalton so he could join the pursuit.

"Copy that," replied the Texan, his tone now also serious, but with a hint of excitement.

Kryton stood up, gained his balance, and started running.

12

Kryton moved at speed along the tiled roof and to the edge where he had seen the Chinese man jump down. He cautiously looked over, pistol extended and ready to engage.

There was nothing at the bottom of the house except a few bins. He looked up and saw the Chinese man running up the alleyway. Kryton lowered himself into the alleyway; he wasn't convinced his knees would appreciate another jump from that height. He started running after the man. The alleyway was littered with a mix of rubbish, wooden pallets and scooters.

The odd dog was forced to jump out of the way as Kryton ran after his assailant.

He saw the Chinese man get to a corner, turn and fire a shot.

The bullet was well off target as the shooter was out of range, but years of close quarter combat training still ensured that Kryton looked for some cover. He crouched down behind a small metal bin and heard the Chinese bullet slam into the wall a few feet from where he was.

He looked back along the alleyway, but the Chinese man had gone.

Kryton raced up to the corner where the shot had been fired from, and rapidly moved around it, hoping to catch the Chinese man by surprise if he was hiding in wait. A Timorese mother was crouched at the front of a small corrugated iron shack, huddling over her two children to protect them.

She looked up at Kryton.

He raised both his hands up to his side, showing he wasn't a threat.

"Dia'k, dia'k," he said smiling, speaking in Tetum to say that he was one of the good guys.

She could see he wasn't a threat and so she nodded in response, her young children with their heads buried in their mother's arms.

He shrugged his shoulders, using universal body language to ask where the Chinese man was.

The mother pointed to a door a few metres up the road.

It led to a house.

Kryton could see drops of blood on the ground leading into it.

He moved quickly, taking a moment to talk on the radio.

"Heading north."

"Copy. Mobile, but hard to move in traffic," came the reply over the radio, Dalton letting Kryton know where he was.

Kryton went flying into the house, ready to engage with his weapon.

A small Timorese man bumped into him, thrown into his path by the Chinese man who was standing in the corner of a small room.

The Chinese man raised his pistol.

Kryton grabbed hold of the homeowner and pulled him back outside through the doorway, just as two bullets slammed into the wall next to their heads.

Kryton heard a mechanical click from inside the house, followed by another.

Stoppage, he thought to himself, meaning that the man's pistol had jammed.

He used the moment to jump back up from his crouched position and enter the house. His aim now was to take a prisoner.

He needed information.

He entered the house, his pistol raised.

A black object came flying through the air at him, and he had just a millisecond to bring his hands up to his face so his arms could wear the impact instead of his nose.

The Chinese man had thrown his pistol at Kryton with his good arm. His injured shoulder had made it too difficult for him to fix the stoppage, making the pistol useless.

The pistol glanced off of Kryton's arms, causing him to lose momentum as he instinctively turned his body to try and avoid the blow. This gave the assailant enough time to dash through to the back of the house, looking for an exit.

Kryton chased after him, weaving through the small kitchen and bedroom of the house and out the other side into what was essentially the backyard. He was now in a small lane that lined the rears of a long row of houses.

A cat scampered as Kryton jumped over a child's bike, with the Chinese man running up the lane.

"Still going north, moving between houses," Kryton said into the radio.

He increased speed, placing his pistol back into his holster in order to improve mobility.

The Chinese man leapt over a small fence at the end of the road, which led down to a narrow drain running east-west.

Kryton followed in quick succession, and by now he was almost on top of his assailant. Out of the corner of his eye to his right-hand side he could see the Landcruiser about one-hundred metres away, moving at speed on the road parallel to, but on the other side of, the drain.

"Maintain direction, you'll see me," said Kryton into the radio as he went down one side of the drain and up the other. He was now on the same road Dalton's Landcruiser was kicking dust up on.

He crossed the road and continued up another alleyway, wider than the narrow lane he had just been on. The road divided a long row of more houses.

He jumped over a set of table and chairs sitting at the front of one of the houses and launched himself at the Chinese man, who had been slowed down by his injury while trying to climb the other side of the drain.

The two fell in a crumpled pile into a small flower garden.

The Chinese man screamed out in pain as he fell on his injured shoulder.

The speed and momentum of the chase was more than Kryton had expected, and he lost his grip on the man as they both hit the ground together.

The Chinese man moved quickly, despite his injury, and was the first of them to return to his feet, immediately kicking Kryton in the side of the head as the Australian tried to get up himself.

The knock rattled Kryton's brain and forced him onto his back.

He recovered quickly, though. Years of playing Australian football and training in martial arts had conditioned him to take such knocks. He stayed low to the ground and turned his body enough to kick out at the Chinese man, aiming at his knees.

The poor position he was in meant the kick was inaccurate, and he struck the man's thighs instead. The force of the blow was still enough to knock the Chinese man back and against the front wall of the house whose garden they were fighting in.

Kryton repositioned himself, trying to get up, but the Chinese man again stepped forward and attempted to kick his opponent. Kryton deflected the blow, but it was enough to force him once again onto his backside.

The assailant went in for another kick.

The sound of a Landcruiser's tyres scraping across the dirt road as it came to a sudden halt gave the Chinese man a moment of pause.

Seeing that he was now outnumbered and losing blood, he jumped back across the small fence of the garden and ran up the lane.

Dalton jumped out of the vehicle and helped Kryton to his feet.

"All good?" the American asked him.

"Yep," responded Kryton, breathing heavily from the chase but more so from the blows he wore. "Let's go."

The two men were about to give chase on foot when up the lane they saw a red Honda off-road motorcycle approach the Chinese man running away. As it got to within a few metres in front of him, the rider applied the brakes and kicked the rear wheel around – a *skid-out* in BMX parlance. The Chinese man jumped onto the back of the motorcycle, and the two of them sped away up the lane.

Kryton and Dalton got back into the Landcruiser and continued the chase.

"This little guy's tough," observed Kryton as he rubbed his jaw.

He didn't think it was broken, but it hurt like hell.

The motorcycle sped through one intersection, weaving between people and animals moving through the alleyways and roads, expertly avoiding all the obstacles that such a narrow space presented.

Dalton increased speed, seeking to close the gap.

He applied the horn frequently, trying to warn people and animals alike to get out of the way.

"These guys are professionals," said Kryton matter-of-factly.

As the two operators were about to cross the same intersection the motorcycle just had, a dog suddenly ran out into the path of the large vehicle. Dalton swerved to avoid the animal, but drove straight into the path of a Timorese man pushing a cart full of vegetables.

The momentum of the vehicle, the fact Dalton wasn't used to driving with a steering wheel on the right-hand side, and the restricted space meant there was little he could do to stop the inevitable.

He applied the brakes, but it was too late.

The cart exploded on impact, sending goods all over the road.

The two men quickly egressed the Landcruiser, fearing and expecting to see someone underneath their tyres. To their great relief, there was just a small man standing next to the wreck, his hands on his head in disbelief and shock.

Kryton looked up the road about one-hundred metres in the direction of where the motorcycle had gone, and watched as it turned right onto President Nicolau Lobato Avenue, merging into the myriad of traffic that was morning peak hour in Dili.

They wouldn't catch them now.

He stood there looking up the road, a steeled resolve in his eyes.

What the hell is going on? he thought to himself.

He went back to where the Landcruiser was. Dalton was unsuccessfully trying to talk to the distressed cart owner using hand gestures. A small crowd had formed, drawn by all the commotion. He then went to stand next to Dalton.

They both watched as the dog that had caused all the mess simply trotted by in front of them, not a care in the world.

Kryton looked at the remnants of the cart, then up at Dalton.

"It would have been cheaper if you'd hit the dog."

13

Dalton drove the Landcruiser up into the front of the complex where the Harbour Master lived. They jumped out and raced up to the apartment. Cav and Carlos were standing in the kitchen, forlorn looks on their faces.

Kryton looked at them, and then over to where the Harbour Master's lifeless body sat propped up against the wall. It was covered in white bandages, and a drip had been inserted into his arm. It was obvious Cav had done everything he could to try and save him.

Not many people survive a gunshot wound to the stomach, though.

Kryton and Dalton joined the other two in the kitchen.

"Catch him?" asked Cav, looking at the side of Kryton's face which was turning a shade of purple from the blow he had received in the flower garden.

Kryton just shook his head.

"Almost."

Cav took a closer look at Kryton and told him that he should get an ice-pack on the injury as soon as possible.

Kryton agreed, but he was more focused on trying to figure out what had just happened.

"I'm sorry about your boss," he said to Carlos, "but we need to work out what is going on. Did he say anything before he died?"

Carlos was very composed; any feelings of fear or confusion in the past twenty-four hours were now turning to ones of anger. Too many of his friends and colleagues were dying, and he was angry.

With Kryton by his side, he felt invincible.

"All he could say was *Il Papa*, and, *the Arab*," said Carlos.

Kryton looked at the other two, but they could only shrug their shoulders.

"What does that mean?" Kryton asked Carlos.

"I don't know," was Carlos' simple reply, "He just kept repeating it."

"We did a quick search of the place and found this," said Cav, handing Kryton a small beige envelope.

Kryton opened the top to look inside, and used his thumb to flick through the large wad of U.S. one-hundred dollar bills enclosed within it.

"Wow," exclaimed Dalton, looking at the notes over Kryton's shoulder.

Think I know how he could afford the apartment, Kryton thought to himself, but not wanting to say so in front of Carlos.

He slowly walked around the apartment, thinking.

He was certain that the Harbour Master had been paid to arrange or assist the smuggling, and that there were some Chinese men involved.

"Did Antonio start to do anything suspicious or out of the ordinary recently?" Kryton asked Carlos.

Carlos thought for a moment, but said that he couldn't think of anything.

"What was he like, as a person and a boss?" Kryton asked.

"He was always good to me. He loved to gamble, but he was not very good at it," Carlos said with a laugh.

Kryton raised his eyebrows while looking at the envelope of cash. There must have been about five-thousand dollars in it. That was significant money, enough to change someone's life in the relatively impoverished country. The decent apartment attested to that.

"Thoughts?" he said, seeking input from the two operators.

"This isn't just criminal activity," said Cav, "far too sophisticated, especially considering the resources required to smuggle arms across open water."

"I tend to agree," said Kryton.

The momentary silence was interrupted by the buzzing noise of the encrypted phone vibrating in Cav's cargo pants. He reached into his pocket, pulled it out and passed it to Kryton.

He walked out to the front of the apartment.

"Yeah Jo," answered Kryton, assuming the station chief would be on the other end.

"Zach, are you back in Dili yet?" she asked.

"Yep, we've been in contact with some Chinese. We're at the Harbour Master's place. He's dead," he informed her.

"Shit," she said quietly over the phone. "Well get back here, we've got information."

"Okay. We've got a body here, what do you want us to do about that?"

"Leave it," she said, "we can make arrangements to have the locals sort it out. We don't want to draw attention to your presence in-country."

Kryton's head dropped as he looked inside and over to where the other three men were standing. He could see Dalton using his hands to animatedly tell the others about their encounter with the cart.

"Ah, yeah. We may need to talk about that. We're on our way," he told her, before hanging up to prevent her from asking any follow up questions.

He placed the phone into his pocket and went back into the kitchen.

"We're back to the embassy, they've got something for us."

All three of them nodded.

"The cash?" Dalton asked.

"We'll take it with us, maybe we can trace the serial numbers or something," he said.

The other three started to leave the apartment. Carlos paused for a moment at the doorway and looked back at his boss lying dead against the wall. He made the sign of the cross against his body – a last mark of respect. He then followed the operators out through the door.

Kryton followed, but also paused at the doorway to look back at the dead man. He looked down at the envelope, and then back at the body.

"Hope it was worth it, mate," he said aloud before closing the front door behind him.

14

"What the hell do you think you're doing running all over the bloody country and speeding around the streets, shooting up bloody people's houses?"

The Australian Ambassador was not happy.

Kryton had returned to the embassy with his team, as well as with Carlos, and reported the events of the past twenty-four hours. Any firing of weapons in an overseas location while on government service needed to be reported back home, and that information always had to go back to Canberra via the Head of Mission.

Doctor Tim Greene was a career diplomat, having worked almost his entire life at the Australian Department of Foreign Affairs and Trade – DFAT. Kryton had worked with many diplomats over the years. Some were good; some were clowns.

He considered Greene to be the latter.

The three men just stood there and took the berating, like disciplined soldiers do.

He turned his attention to Jo.

"We can't let them stuff around here while we're trying to rebuild relationships you lot fucked up."

He was referring to an incident from a few years earlier where it had been exposed in the press that ASIS had spied on the Timorese government during negotiations over a maritime oil reserve.

Although such actions would have had to be approved by the National Security Council, which the head of DFAT sat on and the Prime Minister chaired, Greene didn't seem willing to make such distinctions at that moment.

"Sir, they acted in self-defence, and they had the full authority of Canberra to undertake this operation," said Jo, making an effort to calm the Ambassador down.

He just looked at her in a huff, then back at the men standing before him. They returned his gaze, completely unfazed.

They certainly weren't going to allow themselves to be intimidated by the frumpy little man who looked like he hadn't done his daily fitness workout in quite some time.

Greene looked straight at Dalton.

"You can bet the U.S. Ambassador is not going to be impressed by this," he said, trying to restore authority over the three much larger men.

Dalton stood still for a moment, but the silence made him think the Ambassador was waiting for him to say something.

"Umm, I'm sure he'll appreciate your call, sir," Dalton said in response, showing the usual levels of respect and politeness U.S. servicemen do, even in the face of stupidity.

The Ambassador's aide entered the room, walked over to him and whispered something into his ear. He listened intensely and nodded.

"Jo, we'll sort this out later. As for you three, you're on the last flight to Australia tonight," he said before turning around and leaving the room with his aide. It seemed something else warranted his attention.

The three men looked at each other. Cav just rolled his eyes.

Kryton walked purposefully over to where Jo was standing.

"Jo, we haven't got time for this shit," he said assertively.

"I know," she said raising her arms in a placating gesture, "he's had his vent, so that should be that. Let's go back to the SCIF."

They all returned to the SCIF, where Carlos was waiting with another member of the station, a young female obviously not long graduated from the service's training course.

"Right, so what did you find?" asked Kryton as they gathered around the table with the map on it.

Oakover motioned towards where Carlos was sitting, as if to ask if his presence was needed.

"Hey, he's as involved in this now as any of us," Kryton said, shutting down the Colonel before he could make any other comments.

Oakover nodded in agreement. He realised that the lad still had a role to play in identifying the Chinese men.

"We've asked the Americans about the boxes with the few numbers stencilled on them you told us about," said Jo. "We should hear something soon."

She moved to the end of the table to where a laptop was sitting, opened the cover and played with a few buttons. She turned it around so everyone could see it.

A black and white video appeared on the screen.

The footage showed a gate with a truck behind it. Two Chinese men appeared to play with a small keypad on the side of the gate.

"This is the CCTV from the wharf the other morning," she said.

Kryton looked at her. The corner of his lip raised slightly, suggesting he was impressed.

"Well done," was all he said.

He knew she had talents, but to have obtained the video indirectly in less than twenty-four hours was impressive.

They watched as the men on the video played with the gate lock keypad for a few moments.

"No sound, sorry," lamented Jo.

They continued to watch as Alberto came out of the shadows of the warehouse and to the side of the truck, only to be intercepted by the Boss.

Carlos knew what was about to happen, but he couldn't watch it.

"It's okay to step outside, mate," Kryton said to the young Timorese man, motioning for the other station member to go with him.

He nodded and went with the girl outside.

"Go on," he said to Jo, who continued playing the video.

They watched as the Boss shot Alberto in the back, and then in company with the Driver chase after Carlos.

"Well that clears Carlos," Kryton muttered, breathing a small sigh of relief.

He had never doubted his friend, but this ensured no-one else could either.

They watched the rest of the available video, which wasn't as much as they would have liked, but still better than nothing.

Kryton asked Jo to rewind to an earlier part.

"Can you zoom in?" he asked her.

She played with a few buttons and zoomed in on the face of the Signaller, who was trying to enter the code into the keypad.

"That's the guy with the lead boot," he said while subconsciously rubbing his jaw.

"Can we see further up the wharf to where the truck came from? Perhaps see what or where they unloaded the boxes from?" asked Cav.

"Afraid not, the cameras don't go all the way back there. We're pretty lucky to get this," Jo said as she closed the laptop cover.

"Far from decent security," observed Cav.

Kryton stood up from his leaning position on the table and brushed his palm over his face in thought.

"If the Harbour Master was involved, why didn't he shut down the CCTV?" asked Dalton.

Kryton thought for a moment.

"Those Chinese guys moved quickly, and they only got hindered by the gate," he said. "I don't think shooting a local security guard was part of the plan. They hadn't expected any disruptions or delays. He'd done his part by ensuring there would be no other vessels alongside the wharf that night."

"But the guards could have seen them on cameras if they were watching closely," suggested Jo.

"Maybe. But perhaps shutting it off would have aroused *too* much suspicion. Maybe he was relying on their inattention," Kryton said. "We'll never actually know now, though."

"So why go back to the Harbour Master's place and kill him. It's risky," queried Oakover.

"The shooting was on the news," Kryton said. "They figured it was only a matter of time until the police found him and questioned him about it, so they probably thought that he might give them up."

Kryton leaned back against the table, focusing his thoughts by looking at the ground.

"Better to eliminate him than take that risk. It took them nearly two days to find him, so they must not have known where he lived."

Cav and Dalton looked at him intensely, admiring the analytical process they were watching unfold in front of them.

"That suggests if they were using him as a lackey, it's only a recent thing because they had to go looking for him. That means they didn't have a detailed profile on him. He didn't have much furniture, so it looks like he had just upscaled his living conditions having expected to get a hefty payday from his Chinese handlers."

"Well that also means whatever the Chinese men were doing, it's still a live operation," said Jo. "If they were going to use him only once, then it wouldn't matter what he told the police after the event because whatever they were here to do would have been done, and there would be no need for more secrecy because they would be long gone."

"Exactly," said Kryton.

"So how *did* they find him?" asked Dalton, trying to keep up with the thought process of the two intelligence operators.

"Like Cav said before – resources!" exclaimed Kryton. "As we saw on the street, these guys are professionals. They've had help to tie up the loose ends."

"State-sponsored?" asked Jo.

"Well, we can try to trace the cash we found on the Harbour Master and find its origins. It's certainly possible this is state-sponsored, though."

"I'd say almost certain," interjected Oakover.

The rest of the crew around the table looked at the army officer.

"What is it?" asked Kryton.

"I received answers on your request about Chinese military activity. Your hunch was correct. Naval intelligence reported that a Chinese sub they were tracking south through the Molucca Sea disappeared a week ago. It was headed towards the Banda Sea," he informed everyone.

Kryton dropped his head and sighed. The pieces weren't forming a very nice puzzle.

"Where is the Banda Sea?" queried Cav.

"About a kilometre that way," said Kryton, pointing towards the wall of the SCIF, but actually inferring the beach just up the road from where they were now.

"U.S. Pacific Command also can't find it," Oakover added.

Dalton's eyes widened.

"Shit, you think they used a sub to bring arms into the country?" he asked.

"Pretty much," said Jo, concurring with the SEAL's sentiments.

Kryton stood back and placed his hands on his hips.

"Okay, so we've got a missing Chinese submarine; three Chinese operators loose in the city – one wounded; they've already killed; and, if one of them was a better shot I'd be going home in a body bag. Anything else?" he said.

"The local cops – they'll be looking to investigate surely. It was on the news," pointed out Cav.

"They'll certainly be looking out for two white guys who smashed up a business owner's cart," added Dalton, looking at Kryton.

"Just one," Kryton quipped back, winking at the American.

"The law enforcement entities here are far from quick in their investigations," said Jo. "It will take them a while to get to the point we're at now. They'll eventually find and deal with the Harbour Master's body."

"And Carlos?" asked Kryton.

"Don't worry, we'll ensure the CCTV exonerates him, if they even get that far in their investigations."

Kryton nodded his head slightly while continuing to look at the map.

"So, where are these guys now?" he said rhetorically.

"If they're state-sponsored and they're Chinese, shouldn't we be looking there?" asked Cav pointing to the location of the Chinese Embassy on the map, not too far up the road from the Australian one.

"Yeah, we should look for the truck from the wharf and a red motorcycle. We know that much about them," said Dalton.

"We know that no truck and no red motorcycle has entered or left the Chinese Embassy since the incident at the wharf," said Jo.

"How can you know that?" asked Cav.

"We just do," said Jo smiling, the way some intelligence people do when they've got information other people don't.

Cav and Dalton looked at Kryton, confused.

"I doubt our little show is the only operation Jo has running here. Remember what I said about our national intelligence priorities," said Kryton. "Probably with the help of your spooks, too," he added, looking at Dalton, inferring the potential presence of the CIA.

The penny dropped, and they both realised what he meant. It was obvious the Chinese Embassy was being watched.

"So, what does that mean then?" asked Dalton.

"It's likely high-end special operations," Kryton replied. "Like you said, Cav, too sophisticated for criminals."

"They'll be in a safe house?" suggested Cav.

"It would fit the profile of a NOC operation," said Jo, referring to any intelligence operation conducted using *Non-Official Cover* – by where spies practised tradecraft in the purest form; blending into their surroundings and conducting their activities covertly. "They're heavily compromised now, so they'll likely lay low. We may not find them at all."

Oakover grasped his hands together and rubbed them like he'd had enough of the discussion and the theories being circulated.

"Regardless of who those three men are and their location, we know that there are Chinese running arms into Timor-Leste," he said.

"Looks like they might be," said Jo.

"Well, this becomes a strategic issue," said Oakover succinctly, implying that it was now something that needed to be passed upwards and out of their hands.

He was right.

"That's as far as we go, boys," said Kryton to his support team disappointedly.

They both looked at him, unsatisfied with that conclusion.

They'd had a bite of something interesting, something with a bit of action.

They weren't keen just to walk away now.

"I have a meeting at Timorese Defence Headquarters," said Oakover, shaking the hands of all three of the men before leaving for his office.

Kryton tried not to judge the officer too harshly on his apparent willingness to pass it over to someone else. The Colonel was in the upper levels now, and he had to think strategically. It would be hard for a trained special forces soldier to do that, but that was his role now.

"So, what happens next?" Kryton asked Jo.

"Well, he's right, there's not much we can do now but pass the information back on and await direction from Canberra."

She looked over at Dalton.

"We'll inform your guys through the liaison channels."

Dalton gave the thumbs up. It saved him from having to talk to his own diplomats further up the road at the U.S. Embassy.

"What about Carlos?" Kryton asked Jo, thinking of what was now going to happen to his friend.

"We'll ensure the CCTV gets to the police. That will exonerate him. They won't question his reasoning for running off. He was scared, simple as that," she told him.

"Okay then."

There was nothing more that he could do now.

More to the point, there was nothing more he was allowed to do now. He was still officially working for the government, and he had to follow directions.

He thought about the past few days. Carlos was right to seek him out; this was something bigger than just a murder. Not that that in itself was insignificant, but he had to consider it in an international context. What they had uncovered had potentially regional ramifications, and now there were a lot of lingering questions that would need to be answered.

That job belonged to the professionals of the government agencies, though.

Kryton had fulfilled his role.

So had his support team with the help of Carlos.

He walked outside and joined them in the humid air.

"Now what?" asked Dalton.

"We're done," replied Kryton simply. "You two can be in Sydney having a beer at The Rocks this time tomorrow if you're lucky."

Cav and Dalton both smiled. They had been away from home for a few weeks, and they liked the idea of spending an evening in the bars at the famous tourist area under the Sydney Harbour Bridge.

"And you?" asked Cav.

"I'll take my little friend here back home," he said, slapping the good shoulder of Carlos, who was standing next to him. "Do you think Ana has any of that fish curry left?"

"Oh, I think so. Maybe just some," he said sheepishly.

Jo came out of the office and joined them.

"I'll take Carlos home," he told her.

She nodded.

"There's a flight to Darwin at eight o'clock tonight. You'll be able to get the early morning flight to Sydney from there," she told the three operators.

"Sounds great," said Dalton.

Jo looked at Kryton and smiled.

"Umm, so what will you do now?" she asked him, but in an almost submissive manner.

Her demeanour had changed somewhat.

"Ah, Carlos, come and help CD and me get some water for the trip to your place," said Cav, seeking to give the other two a moment of privacy.

The three of them started to walk off.

"Hey you know what, there's time; we can go back with you and have some of that curry," said Dalton to Carlos, slapping a big hand on the much smaller Timorese lads back.

Carlos looked back at Kryton as he walked away with the two operators, a look of bemused terror on his face from knowing that he would have to spend more time with the brash American.

Kryton leaned over the bonnet of the Landcruiser and watched the three of them walk towards the main embassy building. He then smiled at Jo.

"He's a good kid. I owe him much more than just a visit when he's in trouble," he said sincerely.

She leaned in next to him.

"So, how's it felt been back into it?" she asked him, grateful it was now just the two of them.

Kryton suddenly realised what it was. What the demeanour was.

Vulnerability.

She was letting her guard down.

The others had obviously noticed it too.

"Well, I almost had my head blown off, and my jaw and knees hurt like hell. So yeah, can't believe I gave all this up," he said with a hint of sarcasm.

She lowered her head and chuckled.

He looked at her closely.

"I am glad I came, though," he said to her.

She looked up at him and noticed the sincerity in his eyes. She could tell that he meant that he was glad because it provided the opportunity for him to see her.

She looked back down and smiled again.

She had been angry when he had chosen his career over her, but she had never, not for one minute, believed it was because he didn't care for her.

"How's living in Canberra?" she asked, seeking to disrupt the awkward silence.

"It's still cold," he said, stating the obvious about the well-known weather in the Australian capital city.

"But it's not bad, could be worse places," he added.

"You'd know," she observed, knowing Kryton's service history and the many harsh and hostile places globally he'd spent time in.

"I'm getting posted there next year. Time to do my stint behind a desk," she said.

Kryton smiled.

"Promotion?"

"Apparently. I'm unsure in what part yet," she informed him.

They stood as a cool breeze washed over them, indicating that the afternoon storm clouds would soon be coming in.

"Perhaps we can get a coffee?" she suggested hopefully.

Kryton looked at her, trying not to give anything away.

Any thoughts or any feelings.

"That would be nice," he said.

Their moment was interrupted by the noise of the other three men talking loudly as they walked back to the vehicle. They were carrying a large load of bottled water, a few bags of rice, a crate of fresh milk and some newspapers. It was obvious they had found and raided the embassy's pantry.

They arrived at the vehicle and saw the look of disdain on Jo's face.

"It's the least we can do for Carlos," said Cav most unconvincingly.

Jo just shook her head.

"Get that stuff into the back and hide it. I'm already in enough trouble with the Ambassador," she said, showing that she was willing to play along.

The operators just smiled at each other and at Carlos.

Ana wouldn't have to go to the markets for about a month.

The four men jumped into the Landcruiser.

Jo went to the back-passenger door, and with an outstretched arm shook Carlos' hand.

"Good luck, Carlos. Thank you – for everything," she said, motioning to where Kryton was sitting.

"My pleasure, Miss Jo. Obrigadu," he said, thanking her in Portuguese.

She moved to the front side where Kryton was sitting.

"Drive safe, see you back here in a few hours," she said simply.

He nodded and smiled. He placed a pair of dark Oakley sunglasses over his eyes.

"See you soon."

15

The four men sat in the Landcruiser as it weaved its way through the afternoon traffic in Dili. They all sat in silence in private thought.

"Am I the only one who's pissed we're leaving this alone," blurted out Dalton from the back seat.

Kryton had decided that one busted-up vegetable cart was enough for this trip, and asked Cav to take over driving duties.

The other three laughed and nodded their heads.

The American's statement mirrored their own thoughts.

"We've got three armed Chinese guys wandering around the city; a dead corrupt Harbour Master; and, boxes of weapons that are going to be used for who knows what. Shouldn't we do something?" he added.

Kryton looked over to Cav, who looked back at him with a glance that suggested he also thought that the SEAL was right.

Kryton knew they all wanted to follow it up.

He certainly did.

He wasn't one to hold grudges, but he would very much like to have a chat with the man who managed to kick him in the side of the head.

"Sorry lads, it's out of our hands now," he told them reluctantly.

They drove on a bit further and were soon close to the foothills, which meant the traffic had started to dissipate.

Carlos started to drift off to sleep in the back seat.

Kryton picked up one of the newspapers they had managed to obtain from the embassy. It was a copy of *The Australian*, although a few days old.

He flicked through the pages.

"It says here the U.S. President is visiting Australia next week after he visits Indonesia," he said, turning around to look at Dalton.

"Yeah, I know. I've got to dust off the dress blues and attend a cocktail party at Government House in Sydney. Most of the U.S. military in the area have to attend," Dalton said most unenthusiastically.

Cav chuckled.

"Yeah, mate, must really suck wearing that gold SEAL Trident badge and having to fend off all of the women."

"Well, I never said there weren't positives," said Dalton, rubbing his hands together gleefully.

Kryton looked forward again and just shook his head, smiling.

He placed the paper down in the small pocket in the side of the door. They continued driving.

Kryton looked at Cav, who had somewhat of a forlorn look on his face, seemingly distracted.

"All good, mate? We can't afford another crash," Kryton said mischievously, slightly turning his head to glance in Dalton's direction.

The American kept looking out the window, raising his middle finger at Kryton.

"Stupid wheel on the stupid wrong side," he mumbled under his breath.

Cav looked over at his friend in the passenger seat, grinning as he realised that he had obviously been day-dreaming when he needed to be watching the road.

"Yeah, all good. I was just wondering why you would smuggle arms into Timor. I mean, what purpose? Who would use them?"

"All good questions," replied Kryton.

"Would you smuggle them into West Timor?" asked Cav, referring to the Indonesian province that shared a common border with Timor-Leste.

"I doubt it," replied Kryton, shaking his head, "there's no separatist movement there. No customers. Besides, you could drive a sub straight there and just unload them."

"How about the Timor-Leste Army then, perhaps it's a way to source weapons they can't get otherwise," suggested Dalton from the backseat.

"I wouldn't think so," said Kryton. "The Timorese are free to supply their military from any global source not on a banned arms register. China is still one of those markets."

He turned in his seat to face Dalton directly.

"Our Ambassador back there might have been a bit of a clown, but I guarantee he spends most of his day cuddling up to the host government and trying to ensure Chinese influence doesn't take hold here; so that the locals buy our goods instead of Chinese ones."

Kryton looked back to the front and out of the windscreen. A group of school children were playing soccer in a small park in between some houses. The impending rain wouldn't stop them, and their mothers would have to literally come and drag them back home for dinner.

The first drops of rain indicating the arrival of the afternoon storm landed softly on the windscreen.

16

The noise of the encrypted phone rattling in the middle console broke up their conversation. Kryton picked it up and answered.

"Kryton. It's Colonel Oakover. I have Jo with me and you're on speaker. We have information."

His voice sounded serious.

"You might as well put us on speaker, too," said Jo, also with a serious tone.

She would have known that Carlos was in the vehicle too, so it was either low-key information, or it was urgent.

Kryton fiddled with a button, and now his phone was also on speaker.

"Go ahead, sir. We're all listening."

"The Timor-Leste military intelligence liaison had a chat to me at my meeting. About thirty minutes ago they had one of their agents make contact, saying that he just had a Chinese male come into his office with a gunshot wound to the shoulder."

They all looked at each other. Cav pulled the Landcruiser over the side of the road and into a small culvert.

Hope he uses lots of alcohol on the wound, you little bastard thought Kryton, instantly shocked at his instinct to see pain inflicted on his assailant.

"Why did he share that with you?" asked Kryton, the intelligence professional in him being sceptical.

"Because the liaison actually works for me," said Jo, giving away a little more than she normally should about the agents she had on her books. "He's information is always highly credible."

That was good enough for Kryton.

"Where are they now?" asked Dalton excitedly.

For a moment, Kryton thought that he might have to restrain the American from jumping out of the Landcruiser and conducting his own one-man war.

It was a good problem to have.

Despite holding a similar desire, Kryton was a little more restrained.

"Go on," he said to Jo.

"Their agent is an ethnic Chinese who works as a surgeon in Dili. The Chinese Embassy utilise him for medical treatment for their staff. Four men went into his office to get medical assistance for one of them."

"Four?" queried Kryton.

"Correct. Three Chinese, and one man with fairer skin and dark hair."

Kryton looked at Cav, but he couldn't offer any solutions to the identity of the fourth man. Neither could Dalton.

"If they're NOC, why would they go to a doctor used by embassy staff? Wouldn't they have to assume it's compromised?" asked Dalton.

"I'd avoid anywhere like that," answered Kryton, "unless –"

"Unless, what?" asked Cav.

"Unless they're desperate. He must be in a bad way," Kryton said.

It wasn't enough, though, and Kryton knew it. That was something the local police could handle. Should handle. He knew his team had no remit to pursue, despite their willingness.

Despite his own desire to help Carlos get payback.

They still had no authority to be in-country conducting covert military operations. Nothing had been approved from above apart from the meeting with Carlos. They could be accused of conducting espionage if it was found out they knew about weapons smuggling and didn't pass the information on for the local authorities to deal with. Even going to the Harbour Master's home was pushing it, especially with the can of worms it had opened.

"Who do you think the fourth guy is?" Kryton asked into the phone.

"No idea," replied Jo, "the Americans aren't sure either."

"The Arab?" suggested a soft Timorese voice from behind where Kryton was sitting.

"The who?" asked Dalton, confused.

"The Arab. That's what Antonio said to Mister Cav and me before he died."

Kryton reached around the seat to pat Carlos on the knee.

"Good thinking," he said. "Okay Jo, the fourth man might be an Arab of unknown description. No idea to how he fits into this, though."

"Shit – you think," said mumbled voices over the phone. Jo and Oakover were having some sort of discussion.

"Mind letting us in on it?" asked Kryton.

"We got some fidelity on the boxes, too," said Oakover.

"And?" said Kryton, not expecting to like what he was about to hear.

"The Americans were able to trace the boxes to a consignment stolen from a shipment bound from the U.S. to their bases in Korea about six months ago," the Colonel said.

"That stolen consignment was located through GPS tracking, but by the time their recovery team got to where they were, two boxes were missing."

The men in the Landcruiser looked at each other, mortified.

Dalton sighed.

"Happens more than you'd know," he said embarrassingly at his countrymen's blunder.

"Colonel," began Kryton with an air of concerned authority, "what is in the boxes?"

There was a pause on the end of the phone.

They could hear the officer take a deep breath through the intermittent static.

"Missiles – Stinger missiles."

Cav exhaled deeply.

"Faaark," he said, as he sat back into his seat and looked at the ceiling.

The enormity of what they now knew was happening hit them like a freight train. They wouldn't be able to not do anything now. Not when they had this intelligence and a possible location of the men involved in the smuggling of such a dangerous and potent weapon.

They all knew about Stingers intimately. These weren't just some rusty old AK-47's being sold to drug runners. The American made FIM-92 Stinger missile is a Man-Portable Air Defence System – a MANPAD. More simply, they're shoulder-launched missiles designed to shoot down planes.

All three of the operators had seen them in Afghanistan, often hidden in Taliban caches – remnants from when the CIA had supplied them to the Afghan Mujahedeen to fight the Soviets in the eighties.

This was now a massive issue – known MANPADS in the region. The mere threat of their presence could shut down air-traffic for months, destroying national economies.

"What now?" asked Kryton.

"We've informed Canberra on the emergency line. Officially, we've been told we're not allowed to do anything until they can decide upon a course of action. We're supposed to pass this onto the Timorese authorities, and we can assist to guide them from there," said Oakover on the phone.

Dalton scoffed, while Cav just hit his hand on the steering wheel in anger.

Special forces guys didn't like sitting on the sideline, especially when something of this magnitude was happening.

"What have my people said?" asked Dalton.

"We've informed the embassy, but the Military Attaché is out of the country on his way to Jakarta for the Presidential visit, so they're trying to get word back to the States. They've asked us to help," said Oakover.

"So, we do something," said Kryton firmly.

"We're not allowed to," said Oakover.

Kryton raised his hands in the air in despair.

"But –" interjected Oakover, his voice sounding exasperated as he sighed heavily, "I'm giving you an order to do everything you can to locate these four men and secure the missiles."

Kryton looked at Cav, who shook his fist in delight.

"Hooyah," came the sanguine cry from the SEAL in the backseat.

Kryton realised there was still some of the tactical operator left in the Colonel. He hadn't turned full bureaucrat just yet. He knew the officer was putting his career on the line. If anything went wrong, and even if everything went right, he would likely have to explain and justify to his superiors his role in the whole thing, and his giving the order to intercept – even if it was about potentially saving hundreds of lives.

That's leadership, thought Kryton.

A jet airliner being shot down would be catastrophic. That was worth losing a career over, even if it was incredibly unfair that that might be the outcome.

"The U.S. has no assets in place to support. I'll try to muster some assistance from the local Military Police, they have the long arms," said Oakover, referring to the assault rifles the military carried which the local police didn't.

"Jo?" asked Kryton, seeking her concurrence.

There was a small pause on the other end of the phone.

He could hear her breathing deeply. He imagined the thoughts going through her head.

He was asking her to put her career on the line. It didn't matter for him; he wasn't even officially in the army anymore outside of teaching cadets, and they couldn't sack him again. Dalton and Cav would be able use the cover of the Colonel's order to good effect, not that anything would stop either of them from acting now anyway.

For her though, as station chief, it would be her responsibility to take. There would be no hiding it. Canberra would never believe they acted without her concurrence.

At the planning table in the SCIF back at the embassy, she took the phone off of speaker and placed in deliberately next to her mouth.

"Do it."

17

The vibe in the vehicle changed dramatically. The three operators pulled the weapons from their holsters and checked them, slightly pulling back on the slide to check inside the chamber to ensure it contained a bullet.

They expected to go into action.

"Carlos?" said Cav, asking Kryton what they should do with the Timorese man.

Kryton looked over his shoulder to Carlos sitting in the back seat.

The resolve forged into his eyes was unmistakable.

Kryton looked back at Cav.

"You tell him he can't come."

Cav looked back at Carlos and nodded at the young man in solidarity.

"Besides, my Tetum is terrible," said Kryton, "we may need an interpreter."

The men adjusted their kit, ensuring the radios were all still working.

"Where to?" asked Cav.

"Jo said the office was south of the old Japanese airfield, near the shopping centre and furniture shop," said Kryton.

"I know where that is," said Carlos.

Cav eased the vehicle into traffic, then floored the accelerator.

The rain was starting to come in heavier. That worked in their favour, as it forced most of the smaller traffic off of the road as they sought shelter. There were still some motorcycles and animals to avoid though.

Cav turned on the windscreen wipers to help improve their visibility.

"It's really coming down now," observed Dalton.

"Season, weather or terrain!" said Cav smiling, reciting part of the Royal Australian Infantry's creed that stated that Australians fight no matter what conditions they faced.

The vehicle raced through the streets.

They were maybe only a five-minute drive from their target location.

"Will they even still be there?" asked Carlos.

"If the doctor is half-decent, then yes," said Cav. "The Chinese guy will need a drip and possibly a blood transfusion. That should buy us the time."

Kryton opened the front glove box, took some paper and a pen out and had Carlos draw a rudimentary mud map so they could conduct some quick planning.

"Four on three – not the ideal ratio," said Cav after they agreed on how to make their approach into the surgeon's office.

"We have no choice. We have to get those missiles," said Kryton.

It wasn't that they were scared to face those odds. Special forces operators are trained to deal with forces much greater in number than their own. It was simply that based on what they knew, they were about to face similarly trained operators, and their skills would have to be highly focused.

Mistakes could be fatal.

A few minutes later they arrived near the shopping centre. Cav parked the Landcruiser in a small carpark next to a hardware store.

They would move the last fifty metres on foot.

"Carlos, follow us but stay behind far enough in case something happens. Usual drills," Kryton said.

Carlos nodded. He had worked enough with Kryton to know what that meant, and his skills as an interpreter would be called upon if needed.

The three operators moved quickly towards the front of the office, trying to avoid the rapidly forming puddles and staying under the limited shelter. The most committed scooters and people still moved parallel to them up and down the road.

They all still got sufficiently wet.

Dalton split off from the group and jogged up a narrow alleyway by the side of the surgeon's office.

They planned to catch the four men by surprise, and then identify the location of and secure the missiles.

Kryton and Cav pulled the pistols from their holsters and entered through the front of the office. Carlos waited outside.

The foyer was empty. They looked around, looking for any sign of life. Their fingers hovered nervously near the trigger guards on their pistols.

The vibe didn't feel right.

They moved towards a small hallway which they assumed led to the consulting rooms.

"Nothing seen on the right side, I can't get around a fence, coming back your way," said Dalton over the radio.

"Roger," replied Cav.

As the two Australians moved down the hallway, a Timorese man in a white coat came out of nowhere and bumped directly into Kryton.

It was the doctor.

He had a shocked and startled look on his face, but before he could speak Kryton placed his palm over the doctor's mouth and pushed him back into the room he had just come out of, keeping his arm over the man's chest.

He pushed him firmly up against a wall.

The wide-eyed doctor put his arms up by his side, showing submission.

"English?" asked Kryton, whispering.

The small man nodded. Most Timorese doctors were trained in western universities.

Cav stood in the doorway, keeping an eye out up the hallway.

"We're good guys, okay?" said Kryton.

The man nodded again.

Kryton took his palm off of the doctor's mouth, but maintained the pressure against his chest.

"Chinese?"

The doctor's eyes narrowed as he composed himself. He knew exactly why the two men in front of him were here. He let out a hint of a smile.

"Up the hallway, on the left," the doctor informed Kryton.

"How many?"

"One patient, the others went out the back I think," said the doctor.

"Anyone else?"

The doctor shook his head.

Kryton looked at Cav, who nodded that he had heard.

Kryton released his grip on the doctor and placed his hand on the man's shoulder.

"Go outside and lock the front door," he said to the small man, who then scurried out of the room.

"CD, we're about to make contact, possible three tangos out back," said Kryton into the radio.

"Copy, nothing seen here, still working my way to the other side of the building," said Dalton.

Kryton led the two men down the hallway, pistols raised. They moved past several rooms, all empty. As they approached the door at the end of the hallway, they could see bloodstains on the tiled floor.

They looked fresh.

They couldn't hear anything, though.

To the right was an open door that appeared to lead to a kitchenette. The window above the counter had raindrops streaking slowly down the exterior of the glass, indicating they were at the end of the building.

To the left was another consulting room with a wooden doorway.

Kryton stayed just out of view of the room and leaned into the doorway, his eyes peering over the sight of his raised pistol.

Sitting in a large treatment chair facing the other way from the doorway was a Chinese man, a drip in his arm and bandages over his shoulder. Kryton could see that there was no-one else in the room.

He couldn't tell if the man was awake or not.

Kryton leaned back out and stood back to let Cav have a look.

Once he had, Cav looked back at Kryton, awaiting directions.

Kryton pointed at Cav, and then placed his hands up across his chest, giving a choking gesture. He then pointed at himself before making a puppet gesture with his free hand, indicating that he would talk.

Cav nodded that he understood the plan, holstered his pistol and stood in front of Kryton, ready to enter the room.

Kryton placed his free hand on Cav's shoulder and squeezed gently.

The signal to go.

Quickly and deliberately, Cav entered the room and rapidly moved towards the patient in the chair, Kryton right by his side, ready to engage with his weapon if needed.

As Cav reached the back of the Chinese man, he reached over the chair and wrapped his large arm around the man's neck, simultaneously covering his mouth with his other hand and starting to choke him.

The man squirmed, and muffled noises came from behind Cav's hand.

The choke would have been painful enough for the Chinese man, but the instinctive movement of his hands to try and release Cav's grip would have put indescribable pain on his shoulder.

Seeing that Cav had control, Kryton closed the door to the room, locked it, and then walked over to the front of the helpless Chinese man.

Kryton placed his pistol up and onto the man's forehead, placing his finger over his own mouth in a shushing motion.

The man stopped squirming. His widened eyes instantly, indicating that he recognised the Australian.

"Missiles – where are they?" Kryton demanded in a whisper.

He was certain the man spoke English. It would be virtually impossible for Chinese intelligence or special forces operators to work anywhere without such a skill.

Kryton looked up at Cav, who slightly loosened his hand, allowing the Chinese man to speak.

He didn't say a thing. He just looked at Kryton, a look of anger now in his eyes.

Little shit, Kryton thought to himself.

He placed his free hand on the man's injured shoulder and squeezed it.

Hard.

The man started to wince in pain, so Cav covered his mouth again to muffle the terrible noises he was making.

Kryton stopped squeezing.

The man stopped wincing.

Kryton leaned in closer, forcing the barrel of his pistol harder into the man's forehead.

"Where are they?" he asked again firmly.

Tears were now coming from his eyes. There was only so much pain he would be able to take.

Cav once again removed his hand from the man's mouth.

In pain, he looked up at Kryton. His breathing was heavy.

He was defeated.

"Outside, by a truck," he said in reasonably good but heavily accented English.

Kryton looked up at Cav and nodded his head slightly to indicate that he wanted him to release his hold of the man.

As Cav did, Kryton grabbed the man behind the head with his free hand, raised his other arm above his own head, and with an almighty crack he smashed his pistol across the side of the man's head, knocking him out instantly.

Kryton was always a professional, but he took just a little bit of satisfaction from having been able to even the score.

The two Australians moved out of the room and through the kitchenette, pistols raised and expecting to run into the other three bad guys at any moment.

"CD, location?" asked Cav while he and Kryton peered out of the window and into the street.

"I'm by the side of the shopping centre, it's blocked off as well," he replied.

"Head back and grab the Landcruiser and drive to the front of the office with Carlos," said Cav.

"Copy."

The rain had now eased somewhat. Kryton and Cav moved their way outside and into a narrow alleyway. People, scooters, and animals were moving again, but the sky was still gloomy. Kryton looked up and down the alleyway. To his right about seventy metres away, blocking part of the alleyway, was a small white truck with a green canopy, its front facing towards them. Cav also looked down the alleyway in the same direction. He saw the truck too.

They nodded at each other.

"We have eyes on the truck," Kryton said into the radio.

"Copy," replied Dalton.

The two men started walking towards the truck, one on each side of the alleyway. They hugged the walls and frontages of the shops and houses that enveloped it, maintaining eyes on the truck.

Cav on the left, Kryton on the right.

They held their weapons close to their side so as not to alarm the myriad of people now walking up and down the alleyway.

Suddenly, another Chinese man appeared in the alleyway, coming into view from around behind the back of the truck. He leaned down to check the rear tyre, manipulating a spanner, obviously tightening the bolts on the wheel.

Kryton and Cav stopped in their tracks and watched him.

That was one – they now wondered where the other two were.

That question was answered in a heartbeat.

About thirty metres in front of them, almost halfway between them and the truck, two men exited a small shop, each carrying a small bag of freshly baked rolls.

They started walking casually towards the truck.

One was Chinese; the other had fairer skin, wavy shoulder-length hair and a goatee. Both were well built.

Kryton recognised both Chinese men from the CCTV footage.

It was the Boss exiting from the shop, and the Driver doing the truck repairs.

He assumed the other man was 'the Arab' that Antonio had referred to, although Kryton noticed that he didn't look Arab, but more Persian.

Semantics meant little at that moment though.

Kryton and Cav started walking with haste towards the truck, weaving between the people and scooters that jostled for position in the alleyway.

If they moved quickly enough, they might be able to catch all three of them by surprise while their hands were full.

The two men moved together deliberately, not taking their eyes off of the target.

"Three tangos, on the parallel road from you, to the north. We're approaching for intercept," said Cav into the radio, keeping Dalton informed.

They wouldn't be able to wait for him; their opportunity was now.

They continued their approach, trying to keep a low profile and seeking to blend in with the crowd.

It was hard with their height and build compared to the local population.

Fifty metres.

Forty metres.

The rain was now a drizzle.

Just as they commenced a quick jog, a small sedan suddenly drove out of a driveway next to Cav.

The driver noticed the Australian at the last moment and applied the brakes forcefully. The small car knocked Cav onto his back.

If the screeching of tyres on the asphalt didn't alert the three men by the truck to the imminent threat, the honking of the sedan's horn certainly did.

Time seemed to pause momentarily.

Kryton looked over at Cav. He was okay, but they had now lost momentum, as well as the element of surprise.

They both looked up and towards the truck.

Looking straight back at them were the two Chinese men and the Persian. The car horn had caught their attention.

They were now facing front-on to the two-armed men in front of them.

The two groups were approximately thirty metres apart.

They just stared at each other for what seemed a lifetime.

A true Mexican standoff.

The two Australians had their weapons out, but there were too many people in the alleyway to engage in a gunfight at that distance.

The other men had no such qualms.

The Driver had managed to remove his own pistol from its concealed holster while on the ground, and he fired three shots in the direction of Kryton and Cav, intended more to buy time than for accuracy.

The loud popping sound forced people to scatter in all directions. Kryton ducked down next to a pallet of crates under the awning of a small café, while Cav shuffled on all fours to behind the sedan's engine block.

The bullets passed in between them, fortunately landing harmlessly down the road. The Boss and the Driver jumped up and into the truck, while the Persian man ran off away up the road before darting left up a narrow lane.

Kryton and Cav moved forward towards the truck, their weapons raised and seeking a clear shot through the crowd.

The Boss leaned out of the window, firing three shots of his own. His elevated height in the cabin of the truck meant his shots were also well-off target. They had the desired effect though, forcing the approaching men to once again seek cover, allowing the Driver enough time to engage the gear stick, and place the truck into reverse.

He floored the accelerator and drove backwards down the alleyway, dangerously but expertly manoeuvring the truck towards the main road about sixty metres away.

Cav managed to find a clear shot and rapidly fired two bullets, both hitting the front grill of the truck, but seemingly not causing any detrimental damage.

Kryton and Cav chased on foot, but the truck was fast opening the gap between them. In less than ten seconds, it reached the main road. The Driver applied the handbrake and turned the steering wheel hard, forcing the several tonne truck to lurch violently to the side as it changed direction ninety-degrees. It was now facing north and up the main road it was now on. The Driver changed the gears and once again floored the accelerator.

Kryton and Cav made it to the corner of the alleyway and were now on the road. They stood there, observing the truck as it gained speed whilst driving away. A few scooters were scattered on the road, having unsuccessfully attempted to swerve out of the path of the truck which had cut them off in its efforts to escape.

"CD, where are you?" Kryton said into the radio.

"Still stuck on the road near the doctor's place, the roads are blocked by traffic," he replied.

"Shit," said Kryton, holding his hands on his hips.

Cav was on his haunches, breathing heavily. He was holding his knee.

"That car knocked me over pretty good, mate," said Cav, obviously in a bit of pain.

Kryton looked around, trying to think.

He saw a young Timorese lad trying to pick up a 250cc motorcycle across the other side of the road, having been forced into the gutter by the swerving truck. Kryton ran over to him, helping the boy pick up the motorcycle. It seemed intact.

Kryton made some crude hand gestures, indicating that he wanted to chase the truck with the motorcycle. The lad saw the pistol in Kryton's hand and realised the much larger man was serious. He handed over his bike. Kryton jumped on, revved the engine and accelerated. He slowed down as he passed Cav.

"Find CD and come after me," he said, shouting over the noise of the urban traffic.

Cav gave the thumbs up.

Kryton accelerated.

His eyes focused on his target which he could see off in the distance. They were getting away and he needed to close the gap.

He got down low on the bike and sped north through the now pouring rain.

18

The stewardess moved up the side of the plane by a series of windows. On the tray she carried were two glasses of scotch with ice, and a bowl of pretzels. She wore a neat dark blue skirt, a vest of the same colour which covered a full sleeve light blue shirt, and had her dark hair tied up in a bun.

Standard uniform for females on special VIP duties in the U.S. Air Force.

She reached an inboard door and tapped three times. She could hear two men laughing behind it.

"Come in," said a jovial voice from behind the door.

The stewardess entered and skilfully held the tray level to the floor while she closed the door behind her. She took a few steps inside the small airborne office and was now standing on a rug that bore the same emblem as the one that adorned the front of the door.

'Seal of the President of the United States.'

"Good afternoon, Mister President," she said politely.

"Ah, good, over here darlin'," said President Jack Lang from behind his desk.

The stewardess tried not to roll her eyes. She hated it when he called her that, but his southern drawl had some sort of charming effect, so she just smiled. She loved working for the President. Tall, with greying hair befitting a man in his late fifties, he was always nice and respectful to the staff, even if he did use the odd inappropriate adjective.

The President took the scotch glass from her hand.

"Thank you," he said with keen anticipation.

He motioned over to a leather chair in the corner of the small office.

"Don't forget the Secretary. He'll need it with this result," he said with a grin.

The stewardess walked the few paces to where another middle-aged man was sitting; shirt sleeves rolled up and his tie loosened around his neck, just like the President.

The Secretary of State just grimaced at his bosses' comments, also thanking the stewardess as she passed him the glass. Secretary Bradley Kingston was also admired by the Air Force One crew. A former fighter pilot who flew sorties in the first Gulf War, he spoke their language.

The stewardess placed the pretzels on a small table next to where the Secretary sat, looking up to catch a glance at the college football game they were both watching on the television screen.

Louisiana State University were soundly beating the Air Force Academy, and the President was letting the Secretary know it. It was their respective Alma Maters, after all.

"Colonel Yates says we'll be landing in Jakarta in two hours, sir," she said, addressing the President.

He looked up at her and nodded while taking a sip from the glass. He gave the thumbs up in acknowledgement.

"Outstanding," he said once he finished the sip, before turning his attention back to the screen.

"Thank you, Mister President," she said respectfully before leaving the room.

Up on the flight deck, the pilot slowly eased the controls to make a slight adjustment in course. Colonel Chuck Yates had been the head pilot on Air Force One for over three years, and was due to take up a senior position in Washington D.C. at the end of the year. He didn't mind, it came with a promotion. It would be his first star.

The first of many, he hoped.

He manually altered the control wheel to slightly alter the pitch of the large aircraft. Once in position, he pressed the button to return it to auto-pilot.

Suddenly, the electronics shuddered, causing the display screens in the cockpit to flicker, then shut down altogether.

The plane jolted, as the auto-pilot switched itself off, causing it to commence a slow descent.

Yates once again grabbed the wheel and quickly regained control before levelling off.

The Colonel looked at his co-pilot, Major John Drake, who returned a confused look.

"Display electronics are non-responsive," said the Major.

"Initiate back-up electronics," the Colonel ordered.

The Major fiddled with some buttons above his head, but nothing worked.

"No response," he replied.

"Engines?" asked the Colonel.

Drake checked the dashboard, before looking out of his window to the right-hand side wings. The Colonel did the same on the left.

"All four operational," said the Major, bewildered.

The Colonel went through the checklist: fuel, weather data, communications, controls, and auto-pilot. None of the displays were working.

Yet the plane was still functioning and flying, so some electronics were still working. Power was still getting to the vital areas.

The back-up altimeter and air-speed readings were also working.

A buzzing noise came from a handset positioned in the console next to Yates.

It was the sound-powered telephone the on-board communication centre used as backup to talk to the cockpit.

"Pilot," said Yates, picking up the handset.

"Sir – COMCEN, we've lost all displays and tracking capabilities," came the voice over the phone.

"Defensive capabilities?" asked Yates.

"No readouts on the system, so we can't be sure of the viability of our countermeasures," the COMCEN informed him.

"Attempt to contact NORAD," instructed Yates, before placing the handset down.

NORAD – the North American Air Defence Command – would be tracking Air Force One as it always did. Yates hoped they might be able to provide some advice.

Drake looked down at a small box in between where he and the Colonel sat. He opened the clear plastic cover and looked inside.

"No signal lights on remote launch station," he said, referring to the flares that the pilots could use as a last resort to counter anti-aircraft missiles. "Possible failure."

Yates' mind raced.

What the hell is going on? he thought.

"Attempt to contact the E4-B," ordered Yates, referring to the Boeing 747 that flew in company with Air Force One to act as an alternate mobile command and support centre – otherwise known as 'the doomsday plane'.

Drake tried both verbal and computer encrypted communications but got nothing. He attempted to contact Air Traffic Control at NORAD himself.

Nothing.

They once again tried to manipulate the buttons on the many computers, even attempting to reboot the whole system.

Nothing.

The COMCEN contacted the cockpit again.

"Sir, all computer systems are down – recommend emergency protocols for potential cyber compromise," the manager of the COMCEN suggested to the pilot.

"Approved – enact emergency protocols," Yates instructed the COMCEN.

"Shit, we're blind as a bat here," said Drake, pressing the alert button to bring a member of the U.S. Secret Service to the cockpit.

Yates pulled up his chart board from next to his seat. It was essentially an old-fashioned atlas with detailed information suitable for pilots to navigate with. Even though the aircraft was fitted with the latest in GPS technology, the pilots still tracked their progress using old fashioned paper and pencil – for emergencies such as these.

There was a knock on the cockpit door. Drake stood up to let the head of the Secret Service detail in.

"Yes, sir?" asked the agent.

"We're enacting emergency protocols for complete computer electronics system failure. Prepare the manual aircraft defensive positions," he said firmly to the agent.

The Secret Service agent's jaw dropped, before his training quickly kicked in and he composed himself.

"Copy, sir. Emergency protocols. I'll alert POTUS," he said before closing the cockpit door behind him.

Drake reached over and locked it. Standard procedure.

"Check the charts. What's the nearest U.S. mission with a viable landing strip?" Yates asked Drake handing him the chart board.

Drake trawled through the pages.

He checked their last known position, then traced his finger down south to the series of islands at the edge of the Banda Sea – the closest land mass.

He then traced his finger slightly to the west, until he saw a large star covering a city, indicating a viable location that could receive Air Force One. One that also had a U.S. Embassy that could enact their own emergency protocols to support such an incident.

"Dili, East Timor," said Drake matter-of-factly.

"Right," said Yates, remaining calm like the professional he was, "I'm taking manual control. Major, commence manual navigation."

Drake pulled a small kit from a closed compartment next to his seat. It contained a stopwatch and a speed-time-distance ruler which would allow him to use a clock and basic mathematics to track and plot their location.

The sound-powered phone buzzed again.

Yates answered.

"Sir, no joy on communications with support aircraft or NORAD. We've even tried trailing the VHF wire to talk to our subs on the emergency communications line. Nothing works."

Yates thought for a moment.

"Alternate options?" he asked down the line.

"We have our VHF radio; it's short-range but it's battery-operated. We can use it on the open frequencies," came the reply.

"Copy. We're heading south to Dili. When we assess we're fifty miles out, attempt to contact the U.S. Embassy there," Yates instructed the COMCEN manager.

"Copy, sir."

Yates slowly turned the large plane until it was heading south-by-south-west.

"Mister President, Ladies and Gentlemen, this is Colonel Yates. Be advised we have commenced a change in course and will be conducting an emergency landing in East Timor," said the pilot into the onboard address system.

He turned to face his co-pilot.

"Time to earn that pay, John," he said calmly.

It would take them less than ninety minutes to reach Dili.

19

Kryton pushed the small motorcycle to its limits as he chased the truck north up the road. The rain had caused many potholes to fill with water, and while the truck could easily plough through them, hitting the wrong one could cause Kryton to come flying off.

With no helmet or protective gear, the consequences would be severe.

He could hear Cav and Dalton speaking to each other across the radio, trying to link up to join the chase.

The Chinese men in the truck accelerated, trying to lose the motorcycle now chasing them. Motorists and pedestrians alike had to jump out of the way as they sought to create space. They continued north, before turning right and heading east, seeking to lose Kryton amongst the lanes and alleyways, then heading north again.

Kryton kept his head low and maintained the chase. He threw his sunglasses off of his head, the darkened skies of the heavy clouds made it difficult to see, although now the rain was running down his face.

He shook his head and attempted to refocus.

He turned right where he had observed the truck go into a lane.

He could no longer see it.

The destruction on the side of the narrow lane was evident, as the small market vendors and their supplies had scattered in all directions as the truck wreaked havoc as it had passed.

Follow the mess, Kryton thought to himself.

"I've picked up Cav, we're three-up in the Landcruiser," Dalton said over the radio, informing Kryton that the rest of the team was now back together.

"Roger, move north towards Lobato Avenue, they're weaving in and out trying to lose me," Kryton said, still giving chase.

"Copy."

Kryton worked his way through the scattered mess on the laneway, shouting at already scared people to move as he passed.

It's not low-profile anymore, he thought to himself as he considered the carnage unfolding.

He couldn't dwell on that now, though. If those missiles were allowed to get onto the open market or in the wrong hands, there was no telling how much damage they could do.

Kryton found a clear path through to some open space, accelerating again. The engine screamed as he pushed the low-powered motorcycle to its limits. As he turned north again, he observed the truck crossing a clearing, watching as a few random goats jumped out of the way.

It would be comical if it wasn't so serious.

Or so dangerous.

The Driver felt the steering wheel shake from inside the truck and looked down at the dashboard.

The truck was losing oil, causing the engine to splutter as the fuel line failed to allow petrol to reach the engine.

Cav's shooting had missed its intended target but had, fortunately, hit something vital after all.

The Boss was getting agitated in the passenger seat.

"Hurry up, there's not much time," he shouted to his subordinate, who was trying to keep the dying truck going.

It was still moving though, and Kryton followed the two men as they smashed through a gate to a storage compound, now heading west.

"We're on the old airfield, heading west," Kryton said into his radio.

Less than a few miles away, Dalton skilfully guided the Landcruiser through another narrow road, honking his horn to make the locals move out of their path.

"Turn left here," Carlos said, pointing to a dusty path that bordered a long row of shacks and huts.

Dalton reefed on the steering wheel, almost kicking the back of the heavy vehicle out as they changed direction.

"Through there, that's the airfield," said Carlos.

The men looked to their right, and between the houses and foliage, they could glimpse a large clearing.

It was the side of the airfield.

"We're parallel to you heading west also," Cav said into the radio.

Kryton kept pressure on the throttle. The tyres felt flat, however. The motorcycle hadn't been designed to do the things he had been doing to it in the chase.

Despite losing oil pressure, the truck was able to maintain its distance from the pursuing Australian.

"Go for a cut off at the end of the airfield," Kryton said.

Carlos sat forward in his seat.

"There!" he exclaimed, pointing through the bushes and huts.

To their right, they could see the motorcycle making its way along the airfield.

Dalton floored the accelerator. The Landcruiser bounced through potholes and the generally undulating road.

A mangy cat walked into their path, looking up in time to see the large vehicle bearing down on it. It arched its back, then jumped off into a ditch.

Eight lives left, mused Cav to himself as they sped past.

They were now even with the truck, but would need to gain more ground in order to get in front of it up at the end of the airfield.

The old airfield had too many potholes and divots for the truck to maintain speed, and combined with the loss of oil pressure, it was rapidly starting to lose pace.

As Kryton closed in on the motorcycle, the Boss reached out of the cabin and pointed his pistol at him.

The Chinese man fired two shots. Despite the wind and noise of the engine, Kryton could still hear the whizzing of the bullet passing literally centimetres from his head.

Kryton manipulated the handlebars so that he was directly behind the truck, preventing the Boss from being able to see him.

"Heading north now," Dalton said into the radio as the Landcruiser veered to face a new direction.

The two vehicles were now on a collision course. Kryton eased back on the motorcycle and came out to the left-hand side of the truck again.

"Two-hundred metres from the edge of the airfield – gun it!" he shouted into the radio, guiding Dalton.

The American steadied the heavy vehicle. They could see the edge of the airfield where the tree line on the road they were now on opened up into clear space.

"Buckle up," said Dalton as he gained speed.

"We're going straight into them," he said through the radio.

Although the truck was heavier in the rear, the front cabin was flimsy enough that if he could strike them in the front corner, it would disable their motor.

If.

"Roger," said Kryton.

He deliberately manoeuvred the motorcycle out to the right-hand side of the truck, attempting to distract the Driver.

The ruse worked.

The Driver noticed Kryton coming up on the right-hand side of the truck in his rear-view mirror, and he turned his steering wheel to the right to try and knock Kryton off.

Neither he nor the Boss noticed the Landcruiser flying straight at them from their left-hand side.

Dalton had just enough time to see the truck come into view, and was able to aim very specifically for its front left-hand side.

The bull-bar on the front of the Landcruiser absorbed most of the impact, forcing the vehicle to bounce off of the truck. The front airbags deployed, protecting the two operators in the front. Carlos had secured himself in the back with the seatbelt, and though his upper body snapped forward, he was otherwise unharmed.

The Boss' head smashed into the dashboard of the truck due to the shuddering halt. He recovered quickly and looked up to try and work out what had just happened.

The Driver had also knocked his head, but was otherwise okay.

The two operators in the Landcruiser each withdrew a small pocketknife from their belts and drove them into the inflated bags, causing them to deflate immediately.

Kryton slammed on the brakes of the motorcycle, jumping off of it and running over to the Driver's door. He pulled it open with force, only to be met with a foot straight into his face. The Driver had been attempting to kick the door open as the internal lock was damaged, but all he ended up kicking was Kryton square in the nose, which once again knocked him onto his backside.

I'm sick of these people kicking me, he thought as he found himself looking up at the grey sky.

He quickly turned onto his front to pick himself up.

The Driver had managed to change position and drag himself up into the door frame of the truck's cabin.

He pointed his pistol at Kryton just as the Australian looked up at him, trying to bring his own weapon to bear on the Chinese man.

Kryton's heart skipped a beat as he felt genuine fear for the first time in a long time in his long career.

Two bullets slammed into the side of the Driver's head, dropping him instantly.

Cav wasn't going to allow himself to miss this time.

On the other side of the truck, Dalton was struggling to free himself from the deflated airbag. The Boss looked down at the American from his elevated seat and took aim. He fired two bullets, one striking Dalton in the upper body.

He looked for another target and saw the Timorese man standing idly near the back of the car.

Carlos' eyes widened as he looked straight up at the barrel of the pistol now pointed at him.

As the Boss was about to fire, the windscreen of the truck shattered. Cav had sought out another target after neutralising the Driver, and his bullet struck the Boss in the side of the neck.

It forced the Boss to drop his pistol out through the window, and he slumped down in his seat.

Kryton observed Cav slightly adjust his aim, ready to take another shot, just as he had been trained to do.

"NO," shouted Kryton loudly, jumping to his feet.

He ran over to Cav.

"We need him," said Kryton, placing his hand on his friend's back to thank him for saving his life.

The two men ran around across the front of the truck, opened the passenger door and ripped the Boss out of his seat and down onto the ground.

Cav kicked the man's pistol out of the way, and pointed his own at the Boss, standing over him assertively.

The Boss looked at Cav; he knew if he made any sudden moves, they would be his last. He slumped onto his side, holding his wound.

"Mister Zach," said Carlos standing next to the driver's side seat of the Landcruiser.

Kryton looked up and saw Dalton breathing heavily.

He rushed over and made a quick assessment of the American. Dalton was making some unusual breathing noises, and was wincing in pain. He had a single-entry bullet wound just below his chest on his right-hand side.

"Shit mate, hold on," Kryton said to Dalton.

The amicable Texan gave a slight grin, but in reality, he wasn't well.

"Cav, Dalton's hit. He needs you," Kryton said, rushing over to change positions with Cav, who was still guarding the prostrate Chinese man.

The Boss was lying on his side, placing an open palm over his neck and collar bone to stop the bleeding. Cav's bullet had gone straight through the man's flesh, narrowly missing the myriad of arteries and bone in the upper chest. The force of being pulled out of the cabin of the truck had buckled his knees. He wouldn't be going anywhere.

The rain started coming down again, and a flash of lightning was quickly followed by the loud crack of thunder.

Kryton walked over to Carlos to make sure he was okay.

"My neck's sore, but just another day in the office," Carlos said humorously, using a western idiom Kryton once taught him.

Cav had the medical kit out and was tending to Dalton. He looked up at Kryton.

"There's blood going into a collapsed lung. We need help – now."

Kryton nodded, reached into the Landcruiser and took the encrypted phone from its resting position on the floor. Jo had attempted to call several times, but obviously no one in the vehicle heard it ring over the noise and commotion of the chase.

He dialled the embassy. The phone was answered almost immediately.

"Zach," said Jo, answering, "please tell me you've secured the missiles."

"Wait," said Kryton, "I need urgent medical support for Dalton. Lower chest gunshot wound, likely a pneumothorax."

"Okay, we'll get an ambulance as a priority. Where's the missiles?" urged Jo.

Kryton was focused on what was in front of him and sorting that out first.

"One tango KIA; one at the doctor's office who will need to be retrieved; we have one detained. He'll also need medical assistance. The fourth is a Persian man, location unknown," he reported over the phone.

He could hear an expletive coming from the background through the phone line. He thought it might be Oakover.

106

"Kryton," came a firm voice that confirmed it was indeed Oakover, "where are the fucking missiles?"

Kryton couldn't understand the prioritisation of their focus. He had wounded men needing attention, more important than the location of the cargo. He ran to the back of the truck, drew back the green canopy and climbed up.

On the tray in the back were two long boxes. Both were open at the top.

"Carlos," he called out to his friend, who came around the back and peered into the truck. "Are these the boxes you saw?"

Carlos nodded. "Yes."

Kryton kicked a few rags and pieces of plastic in the back of the truck, looking for something.

He placed his ear to the phone.

"One missile only. I say again, one missile only."

This time there was no mistake in the expletives coming through the phone.

Kryton looked at Carlos, who shrugged his shoulders to ask what was going on.

"Jo, what's going on?" he asked.

"Oh shit, Zach," she said, genuine fear in her voice.

"Hang on," said Kryton.

He jumped down from the back of the truck and ran with Carlos over to the passenger side of the Landcruiser to where Cav was tending to Dalton. He stood by the door and turned the phone onto the speaker.

"Go on, Jo," he said.

"The American Embassy made contact, they've got a VVIP plane coming in to make an emergency landing at the airport," said Jo, referring to a Very, *Very* Important Person.

"In this weather?" Kryton exclaimed.

"Get them waved off," said Cav logically.

"They can't. They were contacted from the plane on a VHF radio. The plane's systems are all disabled and they have no electronic navigational or communications ability. They were able to inform their embassy on VHF, but the storm has disrupted any ability to communicate back to the plane. They're coming in regardless," Jo informed them.

That's not good – at all, thought Kryton looking over at Cav, who also looked concerned.

"Who is it?" asked Dalton through shallow breaths. "Who's on the plane?"

Back at the embassy, there was momentary silence as Jo looked up at Oakover, almost questioning whether to tell them. Oakover nodded. Telling them made no difference.

"The U.S. President," she said.

The four men just looked at each other in shock.

"How the hell have they managed that?" asked Cav.

Like the others, he wondered just how rogue Stinger missiles and Air Force One could be in the same place at the same time.

Those questions were moot at this point.

There was a missile missing; a bad guy on the loose; and, Air Force One was making an emergency landing imminently.

"Why would they land here?" asked Carlos.

"Electronic systems on a plane like that don't just fail, so they would head for the nearest, safest airport assuming a threat to the President. They aren't aware of the danger here, though," Kryton informed him, suddenly realising how all the pieces were now fitting together.

He stood back and looked around. He knew exactly what was about to happen. He knew why the Chinese men and the missiles were here in Dili.

Why Carlos' friends had been killed.

Kryton placed the phone down onto the dashboard of the Landcruiser.

He ran around to where the Chinese man was lying on the ground. Kryton picked him up by the shoulder and propped him up against the front wheel of the truck.

The man winced in pain.

Kryton drove the barrel of his pistol into the buckled knee of the Boss.

"Where's he going?" Kryton demanded.

The Boss was shocked. He looked up at Carlos, almost pleading with his eyes for the Timorese man to stop the Australian from continuing to inflict such pain. His eyes changed suddenly as he recognised that it was the young security guard he had shot at on the wharf a few days earlier.

Kryton looked over his shoulder at Carlos, then back at the man. He placed his thumb into the man's wound and pressed on it. Like the Signaller back at the doctor's office, he screamed out in pain.

"Tell me where he is going, or I give my knife to the boy over there and let him get his revenge," Kryton said softly into the man's ear.

The Chinese man looked back up at Carlos as Kryton continued to press on his wound.

Like his subordinate, he too knew when he was defeated.

He moved his eyes to look at Kryton.

"The statue. He's going to the statue."

20

Kryton ran back to the Landcruiser and picked up the phone.

"Jo, how long until it lands?" he asked quickly.

"Soon, maybe fifteen minutes. They've lost all contact with the plane due to the storm. They're coming in regardless," she said.

Kryton looked at Cav, then at Dalton. Cav grabbed his friend by the arm and walked him a few metres away from the Landcruiser to have a private conversation.

The vehicle was incapacitated from the collision – a flat tyre.

"If I leave him, he'll die."

Kryton pulled his pistol from its holster, withdrew the magazine inside it and replaced it with a full one.

"I'll go alone. One missile, one man," he said, slamming his palm onto the base of the new magazine to ensure it was inserted properly.

He released the slide forward to chamber a bullet.

He ran over to the motorcycle, picked it up and jumped on. He twisted the throttle to rev the engine. He rode the few metres over to Cav.

"Tell Jo I'm going to the statue of Jesus," said Kryton, knowing time was not on his side.

Cav nodded.

The rain had eased and the clouds had started to clear. The last rays of the setting sun managed to peer over the horizon.

He was about to pull on the throttle.

"Wait," said Carlos, having been in thought. "Antonio said *Il Papa*. That's the Pope. The statue isn't Jesus. It's the statue of the Pope at Taci Tolu," he said.

Kryton looked at Cav.

"Makes sense, gets them closer to the plane for a shot," Cav said.

Both Australians knew the place well. They had conducted many physical training sessions while deployed in-country with the army, running up the stairs and winding roadway that led to the top of the hill of Taci Tolu, where a statue of Pope John Paul II overlooked the airport.

"Get that backup Oakover was after," shouted Kryton as he placed the motorcycle into gear and sped off.

He manoeuvred the motorcycle away from the airfield, over a small bridge and towards the main road.

He turned left onto Lobato Avenue and turned the throttle fully on the handlebar.

The engine screamed, being asked to give more than it was capable of.

He knew it would take him less than ten minutes to reach the hill.

Kryton weaved through the afternoon traffic, which clogged up the wide roadway. He expertly found the gaps and spaces that allowed him to keep most of his momentum.

He crossed the dry river and sped past the police station on the right. He continued at speed past the airport where he had arrived less than two days earlier.

So much having happened since then.

He continued west, and soon passed the old bus terminal which had doubled as an operating base for Australian peacekeepers years earlier.

As he turned a bend, the beach came into view on his right.

The sun attempted to shine through the remainder of the storm clouds, giving off an eerie glow that would have made for a great photograph.

In the distance, Kryton could see the outline of the statue of Pope John Paul II, silhouetted against the skyline.

The road was clear now, and he approached the base of the hill. A group of boys was playing soccer on a grassy field, enjoying the last few rays of light.

Kryton ducked down lower, trying to become as aerodynamic as possible on the motorcycle.

It started to splutter. The throttle stopped responding.

"Not now, you piece of crap," Kryton mumbled.

The motorcycle carried him another few hundred metres, before it ran out of petrol completely. Kryton jumped off and dropped it onto the ground. He looked at the side of the hill to the long set of stairs. It crisscrossed up the side of the hill, where it took locals and tourists alike up to the top to where the statue and a viewing platform was.

His personal best time had been ninety seconds from bottom to top, but that had been a decade ago when he was much younger, and in his own opinion, much fitter.

He knew of one man who had run a better time, but that man was back up the road trying to save the life of a U.S. Navy SEAL.

Kryton began sprinting.

He launched himself up the stairs, two at a time, but was slowed down by the wetness caused by the rain.

He used the handrail to stabilise himself as he ascended the hill.

"Move. Move," he said firmly as he dodged and weaved around the few tourists descending the hill, not paying attention to where they were going – like most tourists.

He was now about half-way up, and as he ran up a part running parallel to the side of the hill, he could see the outline of the airfield to his right in the east.

He stopped for a moment.

Something had caught his eye. A glint in the distance reflecting the last rays of the sun.

He looked closely at it as he kept running up the stairs, before focusing back on his ascent.

He didn't need to look again. He knew what it was.

A plane – a big plane.

Approaching from the east and clearly making a descent.

Onboard Air Force One, Colonel Yates had full control of the wheel and manipulated the throttle with the assistance of Drake.

The runway at Dili was far smaller than what a Boeing 747 usually required, so Yates would have to virtually be stalling the aircraft as they touched down so that their speed was low enough to be able to stop on the runway.

Any faster and they would roll into the ocean.

Kryton continued up the stairs and was soon at the edge of the road that continued the rest of the way to the top of the hill.

He knew the Persian would be looking for some height to allow the missile enough air to close in on its target.

He was sweating heavily. The combination of the sprint and the lack of acclimatisation to the humid air meant that he was taking in deep breaths. He was trained to overcome that, though.

He continued as fast as he could, drawing his pistol from his holster as he ran the last one-hundred metres to where the statue was, to the left of a small chapel that overlooked the entire city.

The area was now empty.

Kryton approached slowly, looking for a target. There weren't too many places to hide in what was a relatively open space.

He moved around the back of the statue and to the left, expecting to see the Persian man somewhere near the chapel.

He was correct.

Standing by the left side of the chapel, about thirty metres away and facing east, was the Persian man he had viewed briefly at the doctor's office. He was on one knee, fiddling with a long metal tube, trying to set up the firing control system.

The second missile.

Kryton moved forward tactfully, his pistol held out in front of him and aimed at the kneeling man.

"Drop it or I will –" was all Kryton could shout before he was knocked off his feet by someone who had managed to find one of the few hiding places.

He fell forward, breaking his own fall with his arm. The weight of whoever was attacking him bore down on him as they fell on Kryton too.

Kryton turned and saw that another Persian looking man, much larger, had tackled him seemingly from out of nowhere.

The two men were now on the ground.

Kryton tried to shake his attacker off, placing his hand firmly on the ground and driving his opposite elbow into the man's face. This forced the man to turn to his side, giving Kryton enough time to roll onto his back, cock his leg and drive his foot up under the man's chin.

Finally got one back, he thought to himself.

The attacker was now on his back, but quickly pulled himself to his feet while Kryton, on all fours, tried to recover the pistol he had dropped while being tackled.

The large attacker, seemingly with a steel jaw, ran at Kryton and tried to kick him front-on. Kryton parried it with his left hand while still on his knees, then drove his right fist straight into the man's groin.

This forced the attacker's head to fall forward, and Kryton grabbed his heavy beard and pulled him down off balance. Kryton placed his own hand on the man's back, pushing down on it and using it as a platform the get to his own feet.

He looked over at the Persian man with the missile.

The man had finally managed to get the control system set up and was now placing it onto his shoulder.

Kryton could clearly see the outline of Air Force One as it approached the runway. Blue and white paint on top of a silver undercarriage. A large American flag on the tail.

He took two steps forward, quickly leaned down and picked up his pistol. As he went to raise it up at the Persian with the missile, the other man grabbed Kryton's legs and reefed them out from underneath him.

Once again, Kryton was on the ground. He was still about twenty metres away from the Persian with the missile, who was taking aim at the incoming plane.

But now he had his weapon.

With rapid speed, Kryton turned onto his back and pointed the pistol at the large Persian man about to launch himself onto him.

He fired two quick shots into the man's chest, then one into his forehead.

The bullets were not enough to stops the man's momentum, though, and he continued falling forward onto Kryton's body, trapping him momentarily.

Still on his back, Kryton looked across to the Persian with the missile.

He extended his arm and raised his pistol above his head, only centimetres off and parallel to the ground, in the direction of the man.

He looked over his sight. Any shot from that low, and with the weapon on that angle, was difficult.

He pulled the trigger and fired.

21

The Persian man felt a stinging pain in his calf just as he pulled the trigger of the Stinger missile. The crosshairs of his sight had had the full frame of the Boeing 747 in it, but the pain caused his body to shift slightly as the missile left the tube.

Twenty metres away, Kryton heaved the larger Persian off of his body and jumped to his feet.

He ran over to behind where the other man was lying on his side, clutching the wound on his leg and wincing in pain. Kryton looked down at him, pointing his weapon directly at the man's head.

His finger tensed on the trigger of his pistol, but his professionalism kept him restrained.

They both looked up as a circular trail of smoke filled the evening sky.

Oh no, thought Kryton, fearing he was too late.

The missile raced at great speed towards the still descending aircraft.

Onboard Air Force One, Major Drake noticed the smoke trail heading towards them.

"Missile, inbound, ten o'clock," he shouted, his years of training being called into action.

Yates instantly pushed hard on the throttle and banked the plane to the left, trying to reduce the profile size of the aircraft and its engine exhaust in the missiles infrared camera, which would be seeking out a target emanating heat.

"Engage flares, starboard," he said firmly into the internal address system.

Further back in the body of the plane, a young crewman thumped his fist down on a previously concealed round button, instantly releasing a burst of a dozen white-hot flares that shot out of the right-hand side wing, lighting up the twilight sky over the airport.

The job of the flares would be to burn brightly and linger in the sky, attempting to fool the inbound missile into aiming for the decoy instead of the plane.

Once the plane had turned ninety degrees, Yates and Drake simultaneously forced down on the throttle and pulled back hard on the control wheel, seeking to gain altitude and get out of range of the missile.

The four turbine engines of the plane screamed as it began to ascend, desperately trying to create as much space between itself and the flares as possible.

Had the Persian man not been knocked off balance by the Australian's bullet, the sights would have held true and the missile would have continued undisturbed into the presidential plane.

It hadn't, though, and the heat of the flares did their job. The missile veered to the left and smashed through the centre of the twelve flames slowly floating down back to earth.

Having had its senses deceived, the missile continued flying through the sky for another thousand metres, before landing harmlessly with a splash into the ocean.

Kryton stood over the man as they both watched Air Force One roar past them, almost directly overhead, as it headed south into the darkening sky.

He glanced down at the Persian, who looked back up at the Australian with a look of disdain and frustration.

Kryton lowered his pistol – he allowed himself a small grin as he spoke to the crumpled mess at his feet.

"You missed."

22

Kryton stood at the table in the SCIF, looking over a large photo map of Dili and retracing the locations they had been that day. He jotted down some notes, preparing to write up his report.

There was quite a bit of activity occurring around him, as all the military and intelligence members posted to the embassy were tapping away at computers or talking on secure telephones, trying to decipher what had unfolded in such a short amount of time.

Footage of the missile tearing through the sky at Air Force One, taken by a local man on his mobile phone and posted to social media, was being recirculated on the television news broadcasts globally. The banner headlines all had their own interpretation of events – some accurate, some not.

Jo appeared by his side.

"Dalton?" Kryton asked her, not having seen the American – his new friend – since he had left him in Cav's care at the crash site near the old airfield.

"I don't know," she said sympathetically, unable to provide any more information.

"What's happening now?" he asked her.

She sighed. It had been a long day for her, too.

"Well, both U.S. Marine and RAAF F-18's have been scrambled. They will escort Air Force One to *Tindal*," she said, referring to the secluded Royal Australian Air Force base a few hundred kilometres south of Darwin.

"From there, who knows," she continued. "The Americans will probably want to get him back in the air. The back-up Air Force One is heading to *Tindal* also."

"Is that compromised, too?" he asked her.

"Unsure – there's so much we don't know."

"It's a possibility," said Oakover as he approached the table next to where they were standing.

The Colonel looked frazzled – he had just finished speaking to his superiors back in Australia.

"I just spoke to JOC. Most of the U.S. Pacific Fleet is about to be deployed. A destroyer is being routed to the waters off of Darwin and their intent is to get the President aboard a carrier."

"Why not hold up in Australia?" asked Jo.

"They're considering this an act of war. They'll just act insularly now until they can determine what is going on. We've been asked to provide support to the plane, but that's it," he informed them.

"Their embassy is already trying to secure the two surviving Chinese men, as well as the Persian you shot," said Jo.

"Where are they now?" asked Kryton.

"The Timorese have them, but I'm sure that won't be for long," she said.

"I suppose they haven't said anything," said Kryton.

Jo smiled slightly, folding her arms as she leaned over the table.

"Well, the one you whacked at the doctor's office won't be saying anything for a while, even if he wanted to," she said. "But, the other two haven't said a thing. They're definitely professionals."

Cav appeared in the doorway, holding a phone by his own ear and trying to get Kryton's attention. Kryton looked up at him and motioned his hands for some details.

Dalton? he mouthed to Cav.

Cav gave the thumbs up, indicating that the American was going to be fine. He went back outside to continue his call, no doubt speaking to his own superiors.

Jo saw their exchange and looked at Oakover for more fidelity.

"He'll be airlifted out later tonight on a RAAF C-17," said the Attaché.

"I want to be on that plane with him," said Kryton firmly, always concerned about a fellow brother-in-arms.

"You will be. Canberra wants you back there tomorrow for a debrief. They're not happy," said Jo.

He looked at her and dropped his head in mock surprise.

"Don't worry, you won't be alone. We've been recalled, too," said Oakover, motioning to Jo.

"Of course," he moaned quietly.

He knew how it worked. They had just saved the lives of dozens of people, including the President of the United States, but there would be those in the comfortable seats back home more focused on the optics – how it looked publicly and diplomatically.

The three looked at each other.

Their careers weren't their focus. They were too professional for that.

They all had the same thought, but Kryton verbalised it first.

"So, what the hell just happened?" he said rhetorically.

The other two said nothing. They had no answers, only lots of questions.

Terrorism? A state-sponsored attack? A rogue group of operators?

They had no idea.

Perhaps it was a combination of all three.

How had they obtained the missiles? How had the most secure aircraft in the world been reduced to a flying gas can? So many questions needed answering – and fast.

Whatever it was, it was big, and the follow-up would be severe. The Americans weren't going to take it lightly.

Kryton looked at the television displaying the international BBC broadcast. They were already speculating Chinese involvement, based on some very loose reports coming from the Timorese social media.

Kryton rolled his eyes. He was used to the media recklessly reporting on significant events that he had been involved in, but wild guesses only led to big problems down the road.

"Sir," said one of Jo's subordinates to Kryton as he stood by the television, "there's a man outside asking for you."

Kryton nodded and followed her outside. He walked over to the front gate of the embassy.

Carlos stood there, looking very tired.

Kryton looked him up and down. They didn't need to say anything, they could both tell they were okay.

"How is Mister Clay?" asked Carlos, genuinely concerned.

Kryton smiled. After all that he had been through, the young man was still more concerned about the welfare of someone else.

It was a testament to his character. The reason Kryton had made the journey.

"He'll be fine, mate," Kryton said to him.

Carlos smiled. The two men stood in silence, watching the traffic go by in the darkness of the humid Dili evening.

They both took in everything that had happened.

It was at that moment that Kryton realised that Carlos was miles from his home.

"Oh Carlos, I'm sorry, I've got to get a plane to Australia. We can organise someone to take you home, though," said Kryton, walking back towards the gate and gesturing to his friend to follow him into the embassy.

Carlos just raised his palms up to indicate to Kryton not to worry.

"I have my cousin coming and I'm going to meet him at the café up the road, we will go home together," he said.

Kryton walked back over to Carlos.

"Your family will be safe. We've caught all those involved," he said.

"Thank you, Mister Zach. Thank you so much," said Carlos, some tears welling up in his eyes.

The two friends embraced. Kryton felt that he hadn't yet repaid his debt. If anything, he felt that he – and in-turn Australia – still owed the young man for all that he had done. Still risking his life with such a young family to look after.

"My pleasure," was all that Kryton could really say.

He took Carlos by the arms and looked down at him, like the brother he never had.

"Look after that family. I'll be coming back to make sure you are," Kryton said jokingly, but sincerely.

Carlos nodded. He turned and walked off across the road, and into the Dili night.

Kryton watched him for a moment as he walked off.

Toughest little guy I've ever met, he thought to himself.

He turned and walked back into the embassy.

He thought about everything that had happened in the period of only forty-eight hours. Two days ago, he was teaching martial arts to wet-behind-the-ear cadets, and now he was back up to his neck in his former life.

It made him feel something.

Something he hadn't felt in a long time, something he thought he might never feel again.

He laughed when he realised what it was.

Excitement.

The excitement soldiers get when they're using the skills they trained long and hard for. He could feel it in his mouth, and it tasted good.

120

He wanted more. He wanted to know what this all meant. Why he had nearly been killed, yet again. Those questions would have to wait for a moment though.

He had a plane to catch.

23

Jo walked along the lake, pulling the hood of her jacket above her head and tugging on the drawstrings. She knew it would take her a few weeks to re-acclimatise to the cold weather of the capital.

She watched as a pair of black swans gracefully glided across the surface of the water.

She smiled.

It would be spring soon, and the lake would be filled with all sorts of birdlife and their new offspring.

Always a nice time of the year.

Unfortunately, spring also brought the magpies that would violently swoop down at innocent pedestrians and cyclists passing by, as they sought to protect the nests that housed their own young.

She walked further along the footpath and soon reached a small group of shops.

She walked into a café, embracing the warmth of the fireplace in the corner as she removed her jacket. It was one of those places that tried to make its interior look like a homely living room. Books on shelves and lounge sofas scattered between the usual tables and chairs – that sort of thing.

She walked over to a single lounge chair and took a seat. A young waitress approached her with a smile. It had been a quiet morning – the cold had kept many of the usual customers away.

"What would you like?" the waitress asked in a friendly voice.

Jo looked up and thought for a moment.

"Just the usual," she said.

A flat white coffee. Just like always.

"We're all out of skim milk, I'm afraid," said the young waitress with a serious tone, as if it was the biggest of issues.

Jo tried to stifle a small laugh.

"Normal milk will be fine," she said politely.

The waitress smiled happily and walked off.

Compared to the week she had just had, milk was the least of Jo's concerns.

She picked up one of the many newspapers on the large coffee table.

'Americans continue threats of war,' read the headline.

With who, though? she thought to herself.

She put the paper back down.

She needed a break from all that, if only for an hour or two before she had to return to the office.

She allowed herself to get comfortable in the chair and closed her eyes.

It had been a hell of a week.

The sense of national unity that followed the audacious attack on a world leader soon turned into a very public hunt for a scapegoat as politicians and the media, on both sides of the Pacific, looked to apportion blame for letting the attack occur.

As usual, the intelligence agencies were copping the most flak.

Jo had been cleared of any wrongdoing for her part in responding to the events that had occurred in Dili.

In fact, she had been quietly praised by the Director of the service in helping to prevent a disaster. But political masters needed to be appeased, and she was discreetly removed from her position as station chief.

She was given an early assignment to a desk job back in Canberra – and the promotion she was hoping for.

Strange dynamics I work with, she thought to herself as the waitress placed the coffee cup down on the table in front of her.

She looked out the window and across the lake, before picking up the coffee and blowing on it softly to cool it down.

She took a sip, then frowned at the bitter taste.

She missed the coffee from back in Dili.

Her daydreaming was interrupted by the vibrating buzz of her encrypted work phone, which she had placed next to her purse on the coffee table. She reached forward and grabbed it just as it was about to fall onto the floor.

"Hello," she said into the phone.

Sitting on a grass-covered cliff top overlooking the blue ocean, somewhere miles from that café, Kryton looked into the distance while holding a satellite phone in his own hand.

He smiled upon hearing her voice.

"Hey, Jo," he said simply.

She sat up in her chair, surprised by the voice on the other line.

Pleasantly surprised.

"Zach?"

"Yeah. I just wanted to see how you were going," he told her, not really knowing what else to say.

She turned in her chair to face the wall, as if trying to give all her attention to him.

"How are you? Looking to take me up on that offer of a coffee?" she said coyly.

"I…I just wanted to see how you're going. I heard you were reassigned. I'm sorry," he said, genuine empathy in his voice.

She shrugged her shoulders subconsciously. Not that he could see it.

"It's okay. That's the game we play in," she said.

He knew what she meant. He had seen so many good people fall by the wayside of the bureaucracy. He felt she deserved better.

"What happened to you? I didn't see you after we landed back home," she asked him.

After returning on the RAAF C-17, Kryton had been picked up by some unknown men in a black SUV, while Jo had Jonas retrieve her from the airport. She had assumed that he had been debriefed separately and sent on his way. He was a civilian, after all, and had no obligations to the service.

"I've taken some time to myself. I needed to get away for a little bit. You know what I'm like," he said.

She did.

She also knew not to ask more. She respected his privacy, and he was as likely to be sitting in a bar in Vegas as he was fishing on a remote beach somewhere.

That was the reason things hadn't worked out in the first place. His focus was always elsewhere. Always on the job.

But she knew he cared.

It's why he had called her.

"Yeah. I understand," she said genuinely.

Kryton continued to look over the open water.

Feelings weren't really his thing. Not openly, at least.

"So, what's the fallout been like back there?" he asked, trying to avoid an awkward silence.

Jo ran her hand through her hair, then took a sip from the cup.

"Well, the Americans have taken full control of the investigation. We've almost been cut out of the loop, except for an FBI team due in later today. They want to talk to myself and Oakover," she told him.

"Fair enough," he said.

"The news is reporting all sorts of things. Our government has dropped everything else to focus entirely on this. The Americans are ready to strike at anything that sneezes. We still have no real idea of what happened, and who did it. This could get bad," she told him.

She looked at the door of the café as a group of people walked in. It would start getting busier as lunch approached.

"I'm surprised they haven't asked to talk to you," she said to him.

He watched as a lone seagull floated in the soft breeze, observing its surroundings before landing on a spot not far from where he was sitting.

"I'm sure they'll find me if they want to," he said.

She just smiled.

Another silence.

"When will I see you again?" she asked, still feeling hopeful for a positive response, just as she had when they were back in Dili.

He looked at his watch and stood up from where he was sitting.

"I've got a couple of things to take care of first, but I'll be back there soon. I'll call you."

She leaned forward unwittingly, hoping for more.

He could sense it.

"I promise," he added.

She sat back in her chair and allowed herself a girlish grin.

"Look after yourself, Zach," she said before hanging up.

She didn't want him to say anymore, she wanted to hang on those last words.

I promise.

Kryton placed the phone into his pocket. He stood alone for a moment and allowed himself a smile. He was glad he'd seen her again in Dili; he was glad to be able to call her now. To know that she was okay.

He thought for a moment about their brief conversation. About her comments that the Americans would want to talk to him.

He felt almost guilty that he hadn't been able to tell her.

125

To tell her that they already had.

He turned and walked towards a road and up a hill. It led to a large gate with barbed wire all over the top and several armed U.S. soldiers at the front of it. A long fence stretched out in both directions, almost as far as the eye could see. It also had barbed wire all over the top of it.

'Unauthorised personnel not permitted. Lethal force may be used,' warned the large sign on the front. The soldiers waved him through.

He walked between a row of huts before reaching another gate, as heavily secured as the first one he had walked through.

A compound within a compound.

A U.S. flag fluttered in the light breeze above it, as the sun cast its warmth across the cloudless afternoon sky.

He swiped a key card against an electronic panel and went through.

He continued up a series of steps, and through a door into a dark room.

"Ready?" an American voice asked him.

Kryton turned slightly and saw Dalton standing there. His upper arm and chest heavily bandaged. The American handed him a manila folder with his good arm. Kryton had a quick look at the contents, then handed it back.

"You okay?" he asked the SEAL.

"Where else would I be?" said Dalton rhetorically, a look of steeled resolve in his eyes.

There were several very serious looking people standing to the side by the interior wall, looking through a glass panel into the next room. A few wore American camouflage fatigues, while others were in casual business attire.

Kryton, like Dalton, wore the operator outfit.

He nodded.

"Ready."

Dalton handed him a masked hood, and he placed it over his head.

A balaclava – or as the Americans referred to it, a ski mask.

An armed guard unbolted a rusty lock and opened a large metal door. It was like something found in a darkened dungeon. Kryton walked in and the door closed behind him with a metallic clang. He stood in a large, cold, empty concrete room. A small slither of light peered through a vent running along the top of the sidewall. Just enough to provide some illumination.

Very brooding.

Kryton walked to the other side, about thirty metres away.

Sitting on the floor, facing the door he had just come through, was a lone figure. Their legs were crossed and their arms were tied behind their back. A black hood covered the head. Two large men, also with their faces concealed with a mask like Kryton's, stood a few paces behind the seated figure.

Kryton stopped just short of where the figure was sitting and looked down at the pitiful sight. He looked back over his shoulder and observed the mirror in the corner. He knew that people were watching from the other side.

He looked over at one of the guards and motioned for him to take the hood off of the head of the seated figure.

The lightly bearded man with a prominent goatee squirmed as the first natural light he had been exposed to in twenty-four hours pierced his eyes. He turned his head away from the vents, trying to escape the brightness.

A few moments later his vision adjusted, and he looked up at the masked man in front of him.

Kryton returned the gaze down at the Persian man he had shot at the top of the hill back in Dili.

It had taken the Americans four days to secure him from the Timorese authorities, and in that time, he had started to grow comfortable in a Dili prison cell.

The Americans wanted to return him to a state of shock that all captured prisoners usually feel when first detained in combat. It would assist them to effectively interrogate him. Blindfolded, bound in uncomfortable positions and flown in circles in the back of a cargo plane around the Pacific to a remote military facility had helped to achieve that.

He looked frightened and confused.

The Australian knelt, still looking at the man. He decided to remove his mask. He already had the upper hand on the Persian through having shot him, as well as having thwarted the attack.

He now sought to drive that advantage home.

He looked the man straight in the eyes. The Persian looked back at him curiously, until recognition of his captor kicked in.

His eyes widened and his heart skipped a beat. He looked down at the ground.

Kryton leaned forward, not a skerrick of emotion on his face.

Calm, cool, collected.

Like the professional he was.

He tilted his head slightly to regain eye contact. He wanted to ensure he had the full attention of the man seated in front of him.

The pitiful figure looked up at him.

The Australian leaned forward slightly, and a small grin appeared on his face.

"My name is Zach Kryton – we're going to have a little chat."

Zach Kryton will be back…

Please feel free to follow us on social media and provide recommendations and feedback!

INSTAGRAM

FACEBOOK

AMAZON

Please leave an honest review on Amazon. This helps to tailor better content and allows for reader interaction.

Sign up to the reader's group

Biography

Josh Francis qualified as high school teacher before commissioning into the Royal Australian Navy as a junior officer soon after the September 11 attacks in the U.S. A desire to serve on warlike operations saw him resign his commission and enlist into the Australian Army. After qualifying as an infantryman and paratrooper, Josh deployed on peacekeeping operations in Timor-Leste conducting counter-militia operations.

After completing basic and specialist intelligence operations training, Josh completed multiple deployments to Afghanistan and Iraq, conducting duties in conventional and special operations, as well as training roles.

He is the author of the military-themed personal development books *The Camouflage Series*, as well as the *Zach Kryton* series of books.

www.ingramcontent.com/pod-product-compliance
Lightning Source LLC
Chambersburg PA
CBHW070339130626
46556CB00007B/2943